D1079017

THUNDERBIRDS
ARE GO

THUNDERBIRDS ARE GO

PICK YOUR PATH

Falling Skies

**SIMON &
SCHUSTER**

London · New York · Sydney · Toronto · New Delhi

A CBS COMPANY

First published in Great Britain in 2016 by Simon & Schuster UK Ltd
A CBS COMPANY

1 3 5 7 9 10 8 6 4 2

Simon & Schuster UK Ltd
1st Floor
222 Gray's Inn Road
London WC1X 8HB

www.simonandschuster.co.uk

A CIP catalogue record for this book
is available from the British Library.

PB ISBN 978-1-4711-4557-5
EB ISBN: 978-1-4711-6306-7

Typeset in Myriad by M Rules
Printed and bound by CPI Group (UK) Ltd, Croydon, CR0 4YY

Simon & Schuster UK Ltd are committed to sourcing paper
that is made from wood grown in sustainable forests and supports the Forest
Stewardship Council, the leading international forest certification organisation.
Our books displaying the FSC logo are printed on FSC certified paper.

1

"Welcome aboard the Estrella Grand."

The year is 2060 and you're about to set out on the holiday of a lifetime. You're one of the lucky citizens that have managed to secure a guest place on the Estrella Grand – a vast state-of-the-art space hotel! The whole world is waiting to watch the resort's opening ceremony on their screens at home. The luxury space station has been constructed using groundbreaking technology – a nano-construction technique that enabled it to self-assemble within a week. The science is the cause of great excitement, but is not without controversy. Some are concerned that the project is a stretch too far, as the effectiveness of nano-construction is still unproven. One physicist has even been arguing that the launch of such a massive leisure structure could even be a recipe for cataclysmic disaster …

The atmosphere buzzes with anticipation. As the hotel slowly spins into orbit, the thought of a space disaster is the last thing on your mind. You take a walk through the impressive lobby and are astonished by the number of VIPs and famous faces that you pass – it seems that the great and the good from every continent of the world have come to see and be seen on the space station! You spot Kat Cavanaugh, a TV news reporter, with her camera floating beside her.

"There are claims that this hotel is unsafe," she announces. "Anyone care to comment on that?"

You move on. Kat is clearly after a scoop. She rushes around from guest to guest, trying to provoke a reaction. As the music plays and champagne flows, she doesn't get very far. The grand opening is set to be a dazzling success.

A waiter stops by to offer you a drink. You take it, then look up to find yourself face to face with the height of high society – Lady Penelope Creighton-Ward. Lady Penelope smiles sweetly at you, before turning away again. She is charm itself. The lady moves around the room effortlessly, greeting friends and acquaintances, escorted as always by her faithful bodyguard, Parker.

You are just about to walk over to Lady Penelope and introduce yourself, when you observe her ladyship taking a shiny compact out of her handbag. She steps to one side, but instead of powdering her nose, begins to speak into it.

"Good evening, International Rescue."

The mirror is in fact a communicator, allowing Penelope direct access to International Rescue! You watch in fascination as you realize she is reporting in to the Tracy family. Your heart thumps in your chest when you overhear that International Rescue engineer Brains is the proud mastermind behind the construction of the Estrella Grand. You feel a pang of guilt at overhearing what must certainly be classified information, but as a loyal fan and supporter of International Rescue, you make a silent promise to never repeat anything that you've heard.

Crrrr-aaackkkK!

A terrible splitting sound suddenly rattles through the lobby. Lights flicker. The hotel turns on its side and tumbles into a wild spin!

Guests, furniture and glasses are thrown in all directions amidst shouts and screams. When the artificial gravity begins to fail, everyone finds themselves floating into the air. Anything and everything that is not locked down is now weightless.

The hotel commander's voice comes over the address system, telling everybody not to panic, but it is of little use.

"What did I say?" cries Kat Cavanaugh as she floats by. "The structure has failed already!"

You have no idea what has happened to the space hotel, but something is very obviously wrong. You flick your head left and right, trying to work out your next move. Just then you spot a glimpse of scarlet as Lady Penelope floats past you. She is the picture of calm amongst total chaos. As she passes, you see that she is quietly searching in her handbag. It is then that you spot what you think she might be looking for – her glossy silver compact spins in the air, right past your nose. It must have fallen out of her bag!

"Lady Penelope!" you shout, snatching the compact in your fist.

Too late. The lady has already tumbled out of sight towards the lower reception deck.

There is another mighty crack, even louder than the first. You begin to wonder if Kat is right. With Lady Penelope out of reach and the hotel in free fall, you decide to take matters into your own hands. You open up the compact and put in a call to International Rescue. An image of Scott appears.

"You're not Lady P!" he gasps. "What's going on?"

The Tracy boys are more than a little surprised, but there is no time for questioning – they are aware that the Estrella Grand has been plunged into a full-scale emergency! John reports in from Thunderbird 5 to confirm the news that you have feared – a decompression in the hotel's bulkhead indicates that a major structural failure has occurred.

Brains appears in your communicator, flabbergasted at the news. He can't believe that the intel is right, and even if it is, the nanomatrix has been programmed to re-assemble automatically. Your face turns pale – if Brains hasn't failed, there must be a saboteur at work!

"Who are you?" asks John. "Please identify yourself."

Before you can respond, another massive shudder rumbles through the Estrella Grand. Panic sweeps in every direction. The screams are almost deafening. Somebody needs to stop this! Until Lady Penelope can be located, you are the only person on board with direct access to International Rescue. What are you going to do?

If you decide to go after Lady Penelope and Parker, go to 17.

If you think it's better to find somewhere quiet and report in to John, go to 61.

2

STORY ENDS

The office has no other exit. There is nowhere to hide. You pluck up all of your courage, then flip the switch to open the door.

"This is International Rescue. Please stay calm – an operation is in progress."

You gasp in relief. Scott Tracy is standing outside! You recognize the pilot of Thunderbird 1 instantly. You've watched countless news reports showing International Rescue saving lives in high-pressure situations, often when all hope was lost. You step forward and introduce yourself.

"Thank you for all you've done," says Scott. "Parker and Lady Penelope are safe. They are escorting The Hood into the custody of the Global Defence Force. Our priority now is to stabilize the Estrella and prevent further breaches."

"I might have something that could help," you say, offering up the laptop.

Scott runs some quick diagnostics, before pressing a button on his wrist communicator. A hologram of Brains appears above his palm. Projections of computer code begin to stream around him. His eyes dart from left to right, processing every digit.

"This is the saboteur's laptop," he cries. "All I need to do is run a counter programme through the hardware. I should have any further breaches disabled within two minutes."

Scott explains that Alan is already working in Thunderbird 3 to manually push the Estrella back into orbit.

"This situation is under control," he smiles, shaking your hand. "Great job!"

THE END

3

You're out of options. The quickest way out of this chute is to get to the bottom. You cross your arms over your chest, tuck in your legs and go with the flow.

You fall for second after second, rotting scraps and potato peelings raining down on your body and head. Finally, you come to a stop. The food piles up in an enormous mound, then the side of the chute rotates out of view.

"What is that?" you gasp.

Ahead of you is a giant chrome compressor. A horrible queasy feeling settles in the pit of your stomach. Suddenly the floor tips and the food begins to slide towards it. A bad situation just got a whole lot worse.

You begin to wade through the food, battling towards the far wall. When you finally press yourself against the cold steel, you feel a tiny lip in the metal.

"It must be a door!"

You feel along the lip, then uncover a concealed handle. You try it.

The door is locked.

If you want to find a way to break through
the door, go to 42.

If you decide to call Scott and request urgent
assistance, go to 51.

4

"I'm not leaving you here!" you insist.

Scott is courteous, but firm.

"Please board the last escape capsule," he repeats. "I don't have time to argue!"

You hold out Lady Penelope's silver compact.

"Neither do I," you argue. "But I was one of the last people to see Lady Creighton-Ward. Follow me! I can take you back up to the spot. There might be a clue up there that will show us where to search."

"Okay," agrees Scott. "But let me inform the hotel commander first. He needs to account for every one of the Estrella's guests."

Scott speaks into his wrist communicator. There is no reply.

"John?" he asks. "Where's the commander? He is not responding."

"He was attending to an injured guest in the hotel lobby," you say. "But that was some time ago."

John's hologram appears above Scott's palm.

"I have been in dialogue with the hotel commander,"

confirms John. "He was monitoring the evacuation from the navigation deck. Our last contact was just a few minutes ago. I'll try him again."

You wait. But again nothing.

"Great," says Scott. "Now we have *three* missing persons."

"Something must be wrong," you say. "Parker and Lady Penelope wouldn't just disappear into thin air!"

"Neither would an internationally respected space captain," agrees Scott. "John? How long have we got before the Estrella crashes into the Earth's atmosphere?"

"Two minutes," says John firmly. "Alan is on standby in Thunderbird 3. As soon as you are clear of the hotel he is under orders to shoot the craft down. You need to get out of there fast!"

"Scott!" you shout. "Let's go! We've got three people to find."

If you decide to start your search in the lobby,
go to 12.

If you decide to head straight up to the
navigation deck, go to 39.

5

John's image flickers onto the compact's screen. The lights and monitors of the Thunderbird 5 control panel glitter and hum behind him. From its lofty orbit, International Rescue's global command hub can see everything for 100 million miles. Right now, that feels an awfully long way away from the crisis on the Estrella Grand.

"I want to help," you say. "I'm on the inside. I can be of use."

"It is not normal protocol for us to work with other people," John says seriously. "But I guess this isn't a 'normal' situation. Okay . . . and thank you."

You smile, take a deep breath, then climb up to the top of the ladder. You find yourself standing in an empty corridor, in front of a pair of airlock doors.

"Which way do I go?" you ask. "It's pretty lonely up here."

A 3D holographic blueprint instantly appears, with a neon arrow nudging towards the left airlock. You run towards the left door and leap through it, then press on towards the source of the breach.

"The hotel has two hulls," explains John as you run, "an

outer and an inner. You're moving along the bulkhead between them. Oh, and you're not alone – when Alan docked one of our other operatives climbed onto the ship, too. Her name is Kayo."

"Kayo?"

John gives you a hasty update. He explains that Kayo is in charge of security for International Rescue.

"She likes to keep a low profile," he adds.

You are tired from running and the struggle to take all this intel in. Some holiday this turned out to be! You are just wondering if you are going to get to meet this mysterious operative, when a figure in blue body armour soundlessly drops to the floor in front of you.

"Watch out!" she hisses, pointing to a grey box stuck on the wall.

"You must be Kayo," you guess, "but what's that?"

"This device must be the source of our breach," she replies. "The question is – what do we do about it?"

A red light on the box starts to flash. It's decision time.

**If your first instinct is to try and destroy
the device, go to 40.**

**If you think that the smart move is to get
away from it, go to 64.**

6

The space commander looks at you with desperation in his eyes.

"There's a lady in trouble," he urges. "We need help lifting her out of the lobby. Please, hurry!"

It's time to make a tough decision. One life is in danger here, but if International Rescue does not succeed in its mission the outcome will be dismal for hundreds more.

"I'm sorry, sir," you say. "Please ask some of the kitchen staff. I need to excuse myself."

The hotel commander watches dumbfounded as you push past him and make your way back to the lobby. You feel guilty, but inside you know that you have to be ruthless. The rest of the hotel's guests are depending on it.

When you get to the lobby, the scene is even more chaotic than before. You tuck Lady Penelope's compact deep into your pocket, then battle your way through the noisy reception area, towards the main staircase. After ten exhausting minutes, you manage to pull yourself along the sweeping bannister rail, all the way up from bottom to top. As soon as you make it out through the foyer doors, the rest is easy. You climb into the first elevator you find and ride up to the bulkhead deck.

"The Estrella has two hulls," explains John, as you pick your way towards the compartment. "An inner and an outer. The bulkhead connects the two. Its integrity affects the stability of the whole spacecraft."

You look around you for a moment. The corridor is white and bare compared to the luxury of the lobby – the bulkhead isn't usually open to hotel guests. You look out of a porthole and see the shiny scarlet rocket glide past. Thunderbird 3! A yellow dot darts away from it, then looms into view. It is Scott, preparing to dock in the POD. The craft prepares to land when suddenly the Estrella swings to the left. The communicator makes a buzzing sound.

"The hotel's new orbit is too wild," reports Scott. "Docking now is risky. Make your way down to the emergency zone on the main deck. If there's an evacuation, you'll be more use down there."

**If you agree to go make your way to the
emergency zone, go to 13.**

**If you are determined to board the POD now,
go to 24**

7

STORY ENDS

Your heartbeat pounds in your ears like a bass drum as you listen to John issuing directions to the other International Rescue personnel. This operation is fraught with potential risk. It is hard to believe that you could be key to saving the Estrella.

Scott appears on the communicator screen, still at the controls of the POD.

"It is difficult to find a safe place to dock," he says. "The hotel is free-falling so erratically that the POD is struggling to maintain a velocity to match it."

You look at your watch. Time is not on your side. With every passing second, the saboteur is likely to be moving further and further away from the breached bulkhead. You make a snap decision.

"I will go to the bulkhead now," you tell Scott. "Meet me up there."

"You need backup," he replies. "Just bear with me."

But your mind is made up. As you climb up to the top of the ladder, you grow more and more determined. The saboteur could appear at anytime. You know that. And they're not likely to be friendly. You know that too, but decide not to think about it.

You push through an airlock door at the top of the ladder and climb through. You find yourself standing in a white service corridor. The airlock gives you a welcome return to normal gravity. You make your way as fast as you can towards the bulkhead. Every twenty metres or so there is another airlock door to jump through. You run with all your might, skidding round bends and ducking to avoid ventilation pipes. That's when it happens.

"Ouch!"

You catch your foot on an airlock door, and fall forward. As you stumble, Lady Penelope's compact falls out of your pocket. It spins across the floor. You reach out to grab it, but miss.

"What a pretty mirror," murmurs a voice. "Thank you so much! You've just made my job a whole lot easier."

You peer over your shoulder. A thickset stranger is standing in the corridor behind you, smirking from ear to ear. He shuts the airlock door, trapping you inside. You realize in horror that you've just met the saboteur. Your part in this mission is over. You kick and thump at the walls, wondering if you'll ever get out of the Estrella.

THE END

8

You nod to Kayo and wish her luck. You both know what you need to do. You will go and help with the evacuation, while Kayo stays back to destroy the device. If all goes to plan she will be able to escape from the space hotel later in her vehicle. *If* all goes to plan.

"So long!" you shout over your shoulder. "I hope we get to meet again one day."

As you run, you use Lady Penelope's compact to keep in contact with John. He guides you down through the bulkhead onto a service deck that leads to the Estrella's emergency zone. The zone is packed with bewildered men, women and children. You spot the hotel commander, trying to calm his passengers, and Kat Cavanaugh, who seems determined to stir them up again.

"Could this crisis have been avoided?" she asks loudly. "It seems that the world isn't ready for nanotechnology!"

A tall man wearing a grey utility belt guides the reporter towards Thunderbird 3's cargo bay. He moves with such quiet authority, for once Kat doesn't argue. It must be Scott

Tracy, International Rescue's team leader. You go up and offer your services.

"Alan is preparing Thunderbird 3 for launch," he says calmly. "Can you help me get the last few guests on board its cargo bay? We will be departing in two minutes."

The next 120 seconds pass in a flash. Somehow, working with Scott, you manage to help dozens of people find somewhere safe to sit or stand inside Thunderbird 3. Some guests arrive clutching hastily-packed suitcases, others are still in their evening dress, others have babies in their arms. Across the sea of concerned faces, you see Lady Penelope and Parker joining in with the evacuation effort – both as cool as cucumbers. You run over and return the silver compact.

"Thank you," smiles Lady Penelope. "A lady is lost without a mirror in her handbag."

Alan's voice sounds over the public address system:

"Cargo doors are closing. Please prepare for take off. Enjoy the ride, folks!"

Your heart thumps. As the Thunderbird's thrusters begin to rumble, Scott picks you out of the crowds.

"I'm staying down here with the guests," he says, "… so there's a seat going spare next to Alan in the cockpit. It's yours if you want it?"

If you choose to accept Scott's offer, go to 22.

If you decide to stay with him in the cargo bay, go to 36.

9

STORY ENDS

"I saw which way he went. You seal up the compartment. I'm going to catch The Hood," you decide.

Kayo shakes her head.

"You don't know him," she says. "You haven't seen what he's capable of. Colonel Casey's Global Defence Force has been trying to snare The Hood for years! You wouldn't stand a chance. What chance would a hotel guest have over the world's greatest security force?"

"How about the fact that he'll never suspect me," you answer. "I haven't got a uniform. I don't have an International Rescue insignia on my arm. I'm just a regular hotel guest. That will throw The Hood off guard."

Kayo isn't sure. She presses a button on her wrist communicator.

"Brains, Grandma," she says. "I don't know what to do."

"Sometimes you've just got to go with your gut," replies Grandma Tracy.

Brains nods. He also points out you now only have seconds

before the device in the compartment behind you is going to explode.

You start down the bulkhead corridor, following the direction you last saw the maintenance man heading. The place seems eerily empty now. You open up Lady Penelope's compact and make contact with John on Thunderbird 5.

"Brains has networked the International Rescue operating system with the Estrella Grand's computer," he says. "I can now monitor all CCTV on board and track for temperature hot spots. The scanners are picking up a heat source two hundred metres ahead, about to move into service elevator K."

It must be The Hood.

"I need to catch that lift!" you gasp, breaking into a sprint.

You run for your life, but as you approach the service elevator, the doors ping closed. A line of mauve light tracks the lift as it moves up through the decks of the Estrella.

"He's getting away!" you shout into the communicator. "Can you do anything, John?"

"I'm working on it," replies John, "I just need a few more seconds."

Your heart pounds. You watch the line of mauve getting higher and higher. The Hood is slipping away from you! You scan the lift door, then spot a small switch above the frame – the emergency cutout.

You jump up and try to pop the switch with your hand. It is too high.

"Aw . . . come on!" you shout. "This really *is* an emergency!"

You try again and again, but the cutout switch is out of reach. You are banging the doors of the elevator in frustration when suddenly a black boot swings above your head. It activates the emergency cutout in one swift roundhouse kick.

Kayo steps forward.

"I'm an expert in kung fu," she explains lightly.

You both peer up at the elevator display gauge. The mauve light is now frozen in between decks 32 and 33. The Hood is caught like a wasp in a trap.

"Got him!" you shout.

Kayo grins. "For now at least."

Way down the bulkhead, you hear a distant crashing sound. The Hood's device has exploded.

"The breach has been contained successfully," John confirms. "First class work, International Rescue!"

You glance at Kayo and blush, suddenly realizing that he is addressing both of you.

THE END

10

STORY ENDS

You decide to use the power of surprise to your advantage. Quietly and carefully, you pull out the grapple pack that Scott gave you. You loop the thin length of cord around your hands, take a deep breath, then spring out of the recess.

"Identify yourself!" you shout, rushing towards the figure.

The person stands with their back to you. As you get closer, you see that it is a man dressed in a black suit. You lunge towards him, but the man is too fast. Quick as a flash, he snatches your arm and twists it behind your back.

"I wouldn't do that if I were you," he says with a weary sniff.

Parker! You lurch from panic to relief in under a second. You explain yourself to him, then take Lady Penelope's compact out of your pocket.

"I had been trying to return this," you explain, "but now Scott Tracy and I are on a mission to save the Estrella!"

Parker checks out your story with Scott, then releases your arm.

"Sorry about that – didn't realize you were part of the firm," he says. "Right, then! Shall we get this job over with? I can't stand here all day. Lady Penelope's waiting!"

You grin. With International Rescue on your side, you know you can't fail!

THE END

11

STORY ENDS

You head for the left entry and jump through. You find yourself standing alone in a service shaft. An elevator sits empty in front of you with the doors open. As you step inside, sweat pours down your temples. You don't want to have any more unexpected meetings. Without Lady Penelope's communicator you feel vulnerable – cut off from the safety net of International Rescue.

This time you are in luck, however. The service elevator leads you right up to the very top of the Estrella Grand. When the doors open next, you are in the bulkhead corridor. You make your way towards compartment A-9, hoping that Scott will have docked safely in the reconnaissance POD.

You don't have to wait for long. You soon spot him jogging towards you wearing the familiar blue uniform of International Rescue.

"Pleased to meet you," he says. "What's the situation?"

Scott listens intently as you explain how you discovered the saboteur and sent Parker in to assist Lady Penelope. He flicks a switch on his wrist communicator and holographic images of John and Brains appear.

"I knew someone had tampered with the architecture of the ship!" says Brains. "You have restored my belief in nanotechnology."

John nods in agreement.

"I have received further intelligence from Parker," he continues. "The Hood is now the one under pressure. Parker and Lady Penelope have locked him in the storage unit until the Global Defence Force are able to deal with him."

"Why would The Hood want to damage the hotel?" you wonder.

Scott explains that The Hood is actually a successful businessman, who specializes in construction and technology.

"Brains' cutting edge new technology threatens his livelihood. Discrediting the Estrella so publically must be the only way he saw to put a stop to it."

"So what now?" you wonder. "The hotel is still in dire trouble."

"Now we put things right," replies Scott.

"We?" you repeat.

Scott flicks off his wrist projector.

"I brought this," he says, handing you a utility belt to put on. "We wouldn't have caught The Hood without you. Are you ready to join us for the next stage of the mission?"

You click the belt in place. It feels good. "What are you waiting for? Let's go."

THE END

12

You and Scott run single file towards the nearest exit, utterly focused on the task in hand. Somehow you remain calm. You are already learning how imperative it is for International Rescue to stay measured and in control, even when the situation feels utterly out of control. It helps you to think and function more clearly.

"Follow me," you say firmly. "The lobby is this way."

Scott agrees to trust your judgement, but when you finally make it to the hotel's glass-fronted centrepiece, the place is utterly deserted.

"I saw Lady Penelope floating down towards the lower reception deck," you say, pushing your way through tumbling chairs, ornaments and tableware. You make your way towards the lobby staircase. Scott fixes a small chrome grapple hook on the bannister, clips it onto his belt and then follows it down.

"The place is empty," he says, scanning every corner.

John comes up again on his brother's holographic display control.

"You have just over a minute," he says. "We are going to have to make a call soon on how to proceed."

"We are not leaving Lady Penelope here!" you retort.

Scott takes your arm. He reminds you that as operatives of International Rescue, both Lady Penelope and Parker are aware of the potential sacrifice required.

"We have sworn to protect each other," he says. "But there are innocent people on Earth that are currently in danger, too. If the Estrella crash lands in an urban area, hundreds or thousands could be killed! We have to think about them. We should return to the POD."

Just before you turn to go, you spot the door to the kitchens, tucked at the back of the lobby bar. The last time you saw the hotel commander, he came through it and asked you for assistance with an injured passenger.

"Give me ten seconds," you say, dashing towards the door and opening the airlock. You step back into regular gravity, and then cry out in surprise. Lady Penelope and Parker are standing side by side in the corner of the kitchen, rooted to the spot.

"What are you doing here?" you shout. "You need to evacuate! Please hurry!"

Lady Penelope's eyes dance, but she doesn't move a muscle. With one swift, tiny movement, Parker twitches his head to the right. You follow his gaze and see Kat Cavanaugh standing a metre away. Her expression is fixed into a scowl.

"Another one?" she says with a false smile. "Do join us!"

Lady Penelope nods her head.

"It's all terribly boring, I'm afraid," she begins, but the journalist interrupts. You suddenly realize why Lady Penelope and Parker aren't moving – their wrists are manacled to the kitchen shelving behind them.

"What is going on, Kat?" you demand. "Are you the casualty that the hotel commander was talking about?"

Kat nods her head proudly.

"You didn't fall for it," she shrugs, "but these two do-gooders did. As soon as the commander led them to me, I seemed to make a miraculous recovery."

"They're working together," blurts out Parker, "to make the Estrella fail!"

Kat doesn't even bother to deny it. Her face is smug, triumphant as she tells you that the hotel commander is preparing an escape craft for them right now. You think of Scott. He is waiting just outside the door. What are you going to do?

If you decide to call Scott, go to 58.

If you try to free Lady Penelope and Parker instead, go to 65.

13

"On my way," you confirm. You wait for the space hotel to right itself again, then start working back towards the elevator. Suddenly another ear-splitting crash echoes through the corridor, pushing you down onto your knees. You clutch onto a railing, then flip the communicator open again.

"Scott? John?" you demand. "What's happening out there? I thought you had this under control!"

John's face flickers into view.

"There's been another breach," he confirms. "We are initiating a full evacuation. Somebody inside is determined to ruin the Estrella Grand's maiden voyage. Our priority is to get all of the guests out immediately."

You shudder at the thought of the saboteur lurking somewhere on the ship.

"What will happen to the hotel?" you ask.

"Brains is working in the lab now," says John by way of answer. "Brains – do you have anything for us?"

The scientist's voice comes over the audio. You notice that it is trembling.

"Someone has found a way to instruct component molecules of the matrix to 'unbuild' themselves. It's an extremely localized effect, but in the vacuum of space it can be devastating."

"What does that mean?"

Brains pauses for a moment.

"The hotel has been pushed catastrophically out of orbit," he says quietly. "Very soon, it will enter the Earth's atmosphere and crash."

"Wouldn't it burn up on re-entry?" you ask.

"I'm afraid not," says Brains. "The nanomatrix is designed to withstand that kind of heat. Something this large hitting the ground would be a disaster!"

It's time to go. You hurry down to the emergency zone, your head spinning at the prospect of the Estrella's looming crash. When you get there, you see that Scott has come on board to direct the guests onto the escape capsules.

"Evacuate immediately. This is not a drill," repeats the public address system, over and over again.

Guests and staff swarm around you, anxious to get to the line of capsules. Working with Scott, you help every man, woman and child to find a seat.

"All the other civilians are safe," says Scott at last. "The only people I can't locate are Lady Penelope and Parker. Go and climb aboard – I'll deal with this."

If you volunteer to help find the missing operatives, go to 4.

If you choose to follow Scott's instruction, go to 53.

14

You steady yourself against the ladder, wondering how many more breaches the space hotel will be able to withstand.

From the cockpit of Thunderbird 3, Alan surveys the damage. This new breach is on the opposite side of the space hotel. An image flashes up on Lady Penelope's compact screen, showing a plume of air streaming out of a hole in the bulkhead.

"The decompression is stronger this time, so the Estrella's gone into a much wilder spin," he reports. "I'm going to have to adjust it manually. Could be tricky ... even for a pilot like me."

"You might be able to sort this one Alan," you reply, "but we need to get to the source of the problem."

You ask to speak to Brains. As the inventor of nanotechnology and the designer of the Estrella, he has to be the best person to help untangle this crisis. When he appears, he looks tired and drawn – devastated by the desperate turn of events.

Before you can appeal to Brains, the screen cuts to a video clip. You see Scott in the POD, a dot of yellow hovering in the air just above the new breach. Alan explains that Scott is taking a molecular scan of the damage so that it can be analysed. When you cut back to Brains, he looks even more wrung-out than before.

"Even with this preliminary data I can see that the molecular matrix has been unzipped. Something seems to have disrupted it!"

"The question is, what do we do about it?" asks Alan.

When Brains makes contact next, he has moved down to his laboratory. A multi-limbed robot on tri-wheels scoots into view beside him – his assistant M.A.X.. The robot helper reaches out a swivel arm and adjusts the rim of Brains' holographic display goggles.

"M.A.X. has run the molecular scans through the Tracy Island processor," says Brains. "It looks like the building blocks of the hotel's nanomatrix have switched polarity. They're registering a completely opposite status signature."

"What does that mean?" you ask.

Brains looks into the communicator screen. "It means that someone has found a way to instruct the component molecules of the structural matrix to 'unbuild' themselves. It's an extremely localized effect, but in the vacuum of space can be devastating. My technology is sound. This situation was definitely created by someone on board."

Your mind races. If stabilizing the Estrella from the outside is going to be too difficult, maybe you can do something from the inside.

"Someone is poking holes in the hotel," you urge. "I will go to the breached area, seal it off and stop the decompression. The person who did this will not have got far yet – we may even be able to trap them inside the sealed area."

Brains nods his agreement.

"It is a dangerous … but viable solution," he concedes. "John?"

The screen cuts to a view of Thunderbird 5.

"It's our only option," agrees John, "but you're not going in alone. Stay where you are. Scott will come aboard and get to you in three minutes. Alan – dock Thunderbird 3 and start evacuating the guests. Just in case …"

**If you want to press on towards the bulkhead
right away, go to 7.**

**If you decide to meet up with Scott first,
go to 30.**

15

You're not sure if you imagined it, but did the hotel commander just make eye contact with you? You try to convince yourself that it would have been virtually impossible, but an uncomfortable feeling has started to gnaw away at your gut. The POD raises itself up through the lower levels of the docking bay. Scott clutches the acceleration lever and gets ready to pull back.

"Wait!" you shout. "Don't take off!"

Scott looks bemused. "Why?"

There isn't time to explain, you just need him to get the POD down again.

"There's something strange going on," you announce. "Please trust me."

To your astonishment, Scott does exactly what you say. International Rescue is a tight team – putting their lives in each other's hands on a daily basis. You gulp nervously, realizing that Scott has just put himself on the line for you.

The POD docks back down in the Estrella's bulkhead bay. You both climb out of the craft, but when you run along the tarmac, the bay's viewing window is empty.

"Can you tell me what is going on?" asks Scott.

"It's the hotel commander," you say. "He should be up on the navigation deck liaising with International Rescue and the emergency services. Instead I just saw him watching us in the POD."

Scott raises an eyebrow. "What does that prove?"

"It proves something is wrong. Not long before that I saw him on my way out of the kitchens. He came to ask me to help him attend to a lady who was hurt, even though there were dozens of staff all around that he could have asked instead. Where is that lady now?"

"Okay," says Scott. "I see your point. Let's check him out."

Scott puts a call into John on Thunderbird 5.

"Can you do a background check on the hotel commander?" he asks. "My friend here is concerned about his character."

John places his palm on a glowing touchscreen.

"All staff went through rigorous recruitment training," he confirms. "The hotel commander is called Jan Stevenson. Very experienced. All his files are coming up clean, Scott. Brains interviewed him personally during the construction phase."

"Can you pinpoint him on the ship?" you ask. "He can't be more than a few hundred metres away from this bay."

John consults a 3D blueprint of the Estrella Grand.

"Are you sure you saw him here?" asks Scott.

"He was standing at the viewing window," you insist. "I saw him! Just a few seconds ago."

"That's got to be a negative," says John. "Our intel says that Commander Stevenson is currently working on the navigation deck."

Scott breaks into a run. He calls to you over his shoulder.

"I don't like loose ends. Let's go see the commander and get this cleared up."

**If you decide to go to the navigation deck,
go to 26.**

**If you choose to search the bulkhead first,
go to 70.**

16

You decide to take John's lead. From his all-seeing position as space command, he is best placed to guide you through this situation.

"Scott is back on board Thunderbird 3," he says. "You, Lady Penelope and Parker should go up the navigation deck as quickly as you can. Now our 'hotel commander' is out of action, we need you to help stabilize the controls of the Estrella."

You follow John's instructions to the letter. Soon, you are standing together in the central command hub of the space hotel. Vast glass windows on three sides of the navigation deck offer an awe-inspiring view. A sleek line of scarlet appears to your left – Thunderbird 3! Alan's voice comes over the comms feed.

"Preparing for retro burn," he says. "Hold on tight."

Under John's direction, you override the hotel's autopilot and prepare for impact with Thunderbird 3. The vast rocket's manoeuvring thrusters flare. Alan guides his craft into position, then pushes its nose against the side of the Estrella Grand.

Will the Estrella right itself? To find out, go to 52.

17

You snap the compact shut, then stash it in your pocket before anyone else notices. The hotel is in meltdown. Furniture and people spin haphazardly through the air around you, thudding against walls and hanging desperately from balcony rails. Quick as a flash you duck, narrowly avoiding a spinning orange stool.

"That was close," you mutter breathlessly.

Communicating with International Rescue right now is impossible. You can hardly hear yourself think! You decide to act instead.

You scour the lobby, but Lady Penelope and Parker are nowhere to be seen. They must have made their way to the inner decks of the Estrella, probably trying to find a way to save the super-structure. You decide to track them down and join forces.

Getting around however, doesn't prove easy. Somehow, inch by inch, you propel yourself towards the nearest exit, swerving to avoid flying obstacles along the way.

The deck lurches again and you bang into the wall with a thud.

"Ouch!"

The compact clicks open inside your pocket. You can just make out John Tracy's voice above the wails of the other guests.

"The decompression has pushed the Estrella out of orbit," he says calmly, "but we are sending help. Alan will be approaching soon in Thunderbird 3. He is going to use the rocket ship's manoeuvring thrusters to push the hotel back into position. Scott will ride up in the POD to survey the damage first hand. Are there casualties on board? Can you update me on the whereabouts of Lady Penelope?"

You reach out, grab an aluminium ventilation pipe, then cling on with both hands. You don't trust yourself to pull out the communicator without letting go. You heave yourself along the pipe instead, out of the lobby and down towards a strobe-lit corridor.

It is a little less crowded here. You push forward quickly, scanning the faces that float by, mostly waiters and cabin staff.

"Lady Penelope!" you gasp suddenly, spotting a fleeting flash of red.

Her ladyship disappears into a recess. You make your way over to it and discover a discreet service shaft, set into the corridor wall. Inside the shaft there is a ladder leading up to the top of the space hotel. You can just make out Lady Penelope and Parker climbing above you.

"Wait for me!" you cry.

Lady Penelope keeps climbing.

"Charming to meet you," she calls brightly over her shoulder, "but there's somebody I need to talk to first. Please tell the other guests not to panic. Everything is going to be fine!"

You sigh. Lady Penelope doesn't realize that you have her communicator. And from what you understand about the secrecy of International Rescue, it is not something that you can shout out. You'll just have to catch up with her instead.

Slowly and steadily, you climb up the ladder. The shaft is dotted with portholes, throwing an eerie light into the gloom. As you peer out into the emptiness of space, something glides past your eye line – the sleek silhouette of Thunderbird 3!

If you decide to try and make contact with Thunderbird 3, go to 29.

If you want to keep climbing after Lady Penelope and Parker, go to 67.

18

STORY ENDS

You study John's hologram. While he talks, you notice how his eyes are constantly scanning Thunderbird 5's monitors – checking data, evaluating intel and co-ordinating responses. International Rescue's communications hub is a mind-boggling hive of activity. John is the ultimate multi-tasker, a role that he has trained for his whole life. Suddenly you feel like the rookie that you are. You decide to do the sensible thing.

"Kayo," you whisper. "I'm going to help with the evacuation."

Kayo nods in understanding.

"It was only a hunch anyway," she says. "I'll check it out, then go back to the POD. I work better when I'm alone."

In the blink of an eye she has gone.

"That was a good call," says a voice behind you.

Scott puts a friendly hand on your shoulder. He explains that he has done a sweep of all the decks and every guest is accounted for. He breaks into a jog and you follow, all the way down to the evacuation point. The pace is relentless.

Just when you think you're out of energy, you reach the final airlock. Thunderbird 3 is waiting on the other side, loaded to capacity with nervous hotel guests.

"That must be Alan!" you cry, spotting a young blond man with a red utility belt.

Alan gives you a friendly salute, then makes his way to Thunderbird 3's cockpit. Scott shows you to a seat just behind him.

"You should come with us," he smiles. "It's the very least we can do."

Brains comes in on the overhead comms screen.

"Kayo has located the saboteur," he reports. "He slipped away before she could take him into custody, but at least we know why the nanotechnology failed. Kayo will be back at the POD in 30 seconds."

"Your science was good, Brains. It's just a shame some people aren't," says Scott.

Alan flashes you a grin.

"There are still a *few* good guys and girls out there," he replies. "Starting countdown to launch. 5 … 4 … 3 … 2 … 1 … Thunderbirds are GO!"

THE END

19

"I'll pick the left," you reply, hoping Scott didn't detect the nervous tremor in your voice. The eldest Tracy brother is already running away from you.

"Good luck," he shouts over his shoulder. "When you get to the end of the bulkhead corridor, contact me on Lady Penelope's communicator."

"Copy that!" you shout, heading off in the opposite direction.

You run as fast as you can, desperate to fulfil your part in this mission. As you go, all you can hear is the sound of your shoes pounding on the metal floor grilles. A quick glance at the map in Lady Penelope's compact shows that you are nearly approaching the left airlock.

You are skidding round the last bend, when something makes you stop in your tracks – the shadow of a figure standing just up ahead of you!

You slide yourself back into a wall recess, then crane your head forward as far as you dare. From what you can glimpse of the shadow, the person is of medium height and medium build. They could be anyone.

"This is impossible," you mumble.

Who is it? Could they be the saboteur?

If you are ready to risk moving forward, go to 10.

If you decide to retreat, go to 48.

20

You study the doors. Both appear identical, but when you get closer you notice a tiny scratch on the metal of the right entryway. You immediately step through it.

It is a good decision. The door leads on to a service corridor, a gently inclining passageway that will lead you all the way up to the bulkhead. You soon appreciate the sheer immensity of the Estrella Grand – the corridor seems to carry on endlessly, taking you on a circuit around the extremities of the ship. When you get level with the lower decks, you pause for a moment to rest your legs. So far, the corridor has been empty, but you take care to duck into a recess so that you stay out of sight.

That's when you spot it. There is a small silvery laptop on the floor right beside your feet. A small dent in one corner suggests that it has been dropped. You open the laptop up. A holographic 3D image of the hotel infrastructure suddenly appears in the air before you.

"I need to get this to International Rescue," you whisper. "It could be important!"

If you decide to press on and give the laptop to Scott, go to 31.

If you believe that it will be quicker to go back down to Parker and Lady Penelope, go to 62.

21

STORY ENDS

"I'm coming too," you insist, leaping up next to Scott.

This time nobody argues. Alan expertly stabilizes Thunderbird 1, then lowers you and Scott down into the docking bay of Thunderbird 2. The first thing that hits you is the sheer size – International Rescue's primary transporter is off the scale! As well as carrying an interchangeable selection of PODs, there is space to stow large-scale specialist equipment as well as emergency living quarters.

Scott takes you up to meet Virgil. He sits calmly at the flight deck, tracking the course back to Tracy Island. You speed over the ocean, far away from any major landmass.

"There she is," says Virgil, pointing towards a remote island. You spot what looks like a luxury home nestled into the cliffside. You gasp as an avenue of palm trees parts to reveal a landing strip beneath.

"Brains is ready for us," says Scott. "We'll take him back to the Estrella in Thunderbird 1. Hope you're ready for this? You're part of International Rescue now."

Your heart pounds. You have never felt more ready for anything in your life.

"F.A.B. Scott," you reply. "Thunderbirds are go!"

THE END

22

STORY ENDS

"Thanks!" you beam.

"Least we could do," replies Scott. "You made a real difference."

It has been your dream since forever to sit in the cockpit of a Thunderbird. You sprint over to a transportation tube set in the cargo bay wall. The tube whisks you up to the cockpit, a small round chamber halfway up Thunderbird 3. Alan waves you inside.

"Sit down, strap up and then brace yourself," he says. "This baby packs a punch."

As he talks you through the countdown, the thrusters powering Thunderbird 3 get louder and louder. There's a sudden burst of G-force. Suddenly you find yourself thundering away from the stricken Estrella Grand! As the rocket moves through space, Thunderbird 3's wing pylons begin to slowly rotate.

"Why aren't we spinning, too?" you ask.

"The chair is fixed on rails. That way it always stays in the same position whichever way the craft rotates," explains Alan. "Cool, huh?"

It is very, very cool. Your eyes gaze out of the cockpit windows, taking in the enormity and wonder of space. The next time that you look back towards the Estrella, you notice a small yellow craft dart away from its bulkhead. Kayo! Her face appears on Thunderbird 3's communication screen.

"I located the saboteur," she says. "I should have guessed. This was the work of our old friend The Hood."

"A master criminal," confirms Alan. "The Global Defence Force has been trying to bring him to justice for years. Kayo – did you manage to apprehend him?"

Kayo shakes her head. "I got close, but he slipped away from me. Next time he won't be so lucky."

Alan sets a course for Florida, where Thunderbird 2 is waiting. You watch and marvel as International Rescue shows just what makes it the best of the best. Alan maintains a skilful trajectory, then slides open Thunderbird 3's cargo bay door. Scott then oversees a high-altitude handover, carefully lowering guests down into Thunderbird 2. As you pull away from the transporter, Virgil gives you a wave from the cockpit. It's been quite a day.

"So," says Alan, flicking a switch on Thunderbird 3's overhead control panel. "Fancy a mini-break on Tracy Island? I think you could do with a holiday!"

THE END

23

You take a deep breath and try to think logically.

"I'll start at the top," you mutter, "then work my way down."

The doors glide shut, whisking you up to the top of the space hotel. The glass chamber ascends up past the Estrella's central rotunda to a narrow surveillance deck. The views are spectacular. Stars glitter in the inky distance and a blue glow arches gently beneath. You realize that you are gazing at the Earth's atmosphere. Home.

You are mesmerized for a moment, until you are snapped back into the present by the sight of Thunderbird 3 circuiting the hotel. There is an airlock door at the end of the viewing deck. As you approach it opens to let you through.

Ouch! Suddenly you are back in regularly compressed gravity. You pick yourself up off the floor and dart forward, scanning for clues on how to get to the Estrella's control deck. You pass through another airlock every 20 metres or so, as the corridor curves around the core of the hotel. You round another bend, then gasp out loud – someone is running just ahead of you! It is a woman dressed in a blue flight suit. She stops immediately, then speaks into her wrist communicator. A hologram of Brains instantly appears above her palm.

"I've linked up with our new friend," she says. "No sign of the saboteur ... yet. If they're still here, I'll find them."

"Who are you?" you ask.

The stranger introduces herself as Kayo, another agent for International Rescue.

"John didn't mention you," you say.

Brains chips in. "Kayo runs our covert operations. *Nobody* mentions her – at least not to the outside world. You are one of very few live contacts in the field."

"And I'd like to keep it that way," says Kayo. "I hitched a lift with Alan. It's a case of all hands on deck. Follow me!"

The agent takes the lead, explaining that the hotel has two hulls – an outer and an inner. You are walking through the bulkhead between them.

"Kayo," says Brains. "The next compartment is the one that is breached."

That's when you spot it. A small grey box tucked out of sight, with a flickering red light.

**If you think you should seal the compartment
and evacuate, go to 34.**

**If you decide to destroy the box yourself,
go to 49.**

24

Your heart sinks as you watch Scott pull back from the Estrella. Something tells you that you have more to offer this mission – you can't give up so easily! You can appreciate the difficulties that Scott is experiencing, however. The Estrella is caught up in a lop-sided elliptical spin. You remember the lurch the hotel took when you were down in the lobby. You glance down at your watch and read: 20:10. Although it feels like an hour, that was only ten minutes ago!

Something clicks. You flip open the communicator.

"Scott," you say urgently. "The Estrella is falling on a trajectory that loops sharply every ten minutes. If you try again now you should have time to dock and get me on board before the hotel shifts again."

Scott thinks this over.

"All right," he says at last. "I'll give it one more go. Attempting re-entry now. Meet me in the docking bay."

"Copy that," you reply, sprinting down the corridor. There are two doors at the end. One is marked UTILTY DOCK, the other marked DISPATCH DOCK.

If you decide to go in through the UTILITY door,
go to 38.

If you push through the door marked DISPATCH,
go to 44.

25

You watch the hotel commander disappear from sight, but his face sticks in your mind. Wasn't he meant to be down in the lobby helping out an injured guest? You know it is against ship policy for guests to go into staff-only areas, but how could the maintenance man have alerted him so quickly? You turn to Scott, but decide not to say anything. He's got his hands full already.

Suddenly the POD whisks off to the left, away from the breach on the bulkhead.

"Hey!" you cry. "Aren't we meant to be doing the molecular scan?"

"We might have to put it on ice for a moment. Things are about to get bumpy," replies Scott. "There's a meteor shower coming in."

You look up through the POD's angled glass roof. A terrifying battery of rocks are hurtling towards the Estrella! Alan pops up on the cockpit's comms screen.

"You need to get out of range," he says. "Scrap the scan and come back on board. Let's focus on getting the Estrella back in orbit and out of this rock shower."

Scott isn't convinced. Without the molecular scan, Brains can't work out what is happening to the hotel's nanostructure.

Bang! A tennis ball sized lump of space rock bounces off the POD's probe. You need to act now.

If you persuade Scott to push on with the scan, go to 59.

If you decide it's safer to get on board Thunderbird 3 now, go to 63.

26

STORY ENDS

You and Scott make your way down through the heart of the space hotel, towards the central navigation deck. This is where you would expect a commander to be in a time of crisis – managing his staff and ensuring the safety of the passengers.

You follow Scott through the doors to the control centre, your heart racing with adrenalin. The chamber is a mass of cutting edge technology – state of the art computers glitter, radar screens pip and 3D holographic displays chart the Estrella's reeling orbit from every angle.

"This way," says Scott, beckoning over his shoulder.

He leads you to a central observation platform flanked by a tight group of senior personnel. A man in decorated purple uniform turns to face you – Commander Jan Stevenson. He reaches forward and shakes Scott's hand.

"International Rescue," he says. "Thank you so much for coming. What's the plan of action? The Estrella Grand's maiden voyage cannot end in disaster!"

Scott steps forward to talk to the man, leaving you alone

and miserable. Your wild goose chase has put the whole mission in jeopardy! Instead of capturing the molecular data that Brains so urgently needs, Scott is now tied up reassuring the hotel commander. You vow to never trust a silly hunch again.

As soon as Scott has finished speaking, you step forward to apologise to him. You introduce yourself to the hotel commander, and enquire about the female that was injured in the lobby.

"Casualty?" asks Commander Stevenson.

He seems genuinely confused.

"The lady that needed assistance," you repeat. "You asked me to help you."

The hotel commander shakes his head.

"There are no casualties reported yet," he insists. "And with all due respect, I don't think we've met?"

Scott takes me to one side.

"You were right," he says grimly. "Looks like there is somebody else on board the Estrella masquerading as the commander. This sounds like the work of The Hood. He is a master of disguise. We should have searched the bulkhead first! That's our last positive sighting. "

"Let's get back up there," you suggest.

"We took the wrong call," replies Scott. "The Hood never stands still. We'd have more luck finding a needle in a haystack. We've got to face it – our role in this mission has reached a dead-end."

THE END

27

STORY ENDS

"Follow me," you insist, breaking into a run.

Scott follows you back down through the bulkhead, into the service corridor where you found the laptop. There have to be some clues here to The Hood's next move. As you run, Scott uses a handheld remote controller to scan for foreign devices.

"It was here," you gasp, stopping at the point where you first found the laptop. At least you *think* it was here that you found it. The corridor is so empty and grey it is hard to place your location exactly. Every recess, ledge and air-con pipe looks identical to the one before it.

You and Scott search all around the area, wasting valuable seconds. Nothing comes up. You are about to suggest moving further down towards the lower decks when you feel it – a terrible lurch as the floor moves from underneath you! You hear the sound of rushing air further up the corridor. A single airlock door protects you from another surge of decompression.

John appears on Scott's wrist communicator.

"We have incurred a second breach," he confirms. "Start an emergency evacuation immediately. International Rescue, we have a situation."

Your cheeks flush with disappointment. You made the wrong call. Now you can only hope that Scott, John and the rest of the Tracy brothers will be able to put things right.

THE END

28

You make a split second decision. It's time to get out of here ... now! You run as fast as you can through the hotel kitchens, clattering past stacks of plates, prep stations and huge, commercial ovens. You sprint so hard it gives you a stitch. You lean against a tall chrome fridge and try to catch your breath.

"Psst!"

A hand reaches out of nowhere and grabs you by the arm. The fridge door opens and you find yourself being dragged into the shadows. You fight back ... until you realize that the hand belongs to Parker, Lady Penelope's bodyguard. You give him a hurried debrief.

"Lady Penelope is back there," you tell him. "But take care! The hotel commander isn't what he seems to be. He's taken her hostage!"

"That isn't the hotel commander," replies Parker. "It's The Hood. Most notorious crook this side of the East End! He's the saboteur that's causing all this trouble. Don't worry youngster, I'll sort him out."

"You better take this," you say, reaching into your pocket.

You hand back Lady Penelope's compact, then recount your conversation with International Rescue. Parker disappears back into the kitchens, leaving you to go and find Scott.

This time you decide to stay in the staff-only areas of the ship. The service corridors and elevators are likely to be quieter and less crowded. There are two sets of automated doors at the rear exit of the kitchen. You need to choose one and get on your way.

If you decide to take the left door, go to 11.

If you decide to take the right door, go to 20.

29

You watch Thunderbird 3 cruise past the porthole window, rotating gently in the darkness. Although it appears to be moving in slow motion, the glare of flames blasting out of its thrusters tells a different story. In order to keep up with the Estrella's free fall, the space rocket is forced to travel at a breathtaking velocity.

You slip your hand through the ladder, then pull out Lady Penelope's compact.

"Thunderbird 3," you say urgently. "Do you read me?"

Alan Tracy's image appears in the mirror. You quickly explain who you are and offer your services to the rescue mission.

"Thanks, but I've got this," he says.

Alan pushes Thunderbird 3's thrusters up to the max. The rocket pushes against the Estrella, skilfully using force to stop its wild spin.

"Great work!" you say, as the gravity returns to normal again.

Alan can't resist a grin. "Pretty impressive, don't you think?"

It's a short-lived moment of glory. The space station lists

almost immediately then plunges back into free fall. There's been another breach!

"Time to think again," you say. "International Rescue, we have a situation!"

If you have the courage to seek out the breach and put a stop to it, go to 5.

If you decide to get some advice from Brains first, go to 14.

30

You wait anxiously for three more minutes. At last a voice shouts down from above.

"Scott Tracy here! Climb up and meet me at the top."

You scale the ladder as fast as you can. When you get to the top, a strong hand reaches down and helps to pull you through an airlock door. When the door closes, you find yourself back in normal gravity again, standing face to face with the pilot of Thunderbird 1.

Scott shows you a 3D map of the Estrella Grand. Once you have orientated yourself, he explains briefly that the hotel has two hulls – an inner and an outer. The bulkhead links the two.

"The breach is here," says Scott, indicating a flashing red dot. "There are reinforced airlock doors at each end of the bulkhead corridor. When we get close, we'll split up and then synchronize our approach so that we can seal both ends off simultaneously."

"Got it," you say, nervously repeating the plan back to him.

Scott hands you a utility belt to put on. It contains a grapple pack, an LED spotlight and a trauma kit.

"So . . ." he says. "Which entrance do you want to take? Left or right?"

If you decide to take the left approach, go to 19.

If you decide to take the right, go to 46.

31

You scramble to your feet, tucking the laptop under your arm. You push along the corridor with renewed energy. Adrenalin powers through your veins, overcoming the exhaustion in your legs. At last you reach the bulkhead – a long series of compartments that connect the Estrella's inner and outer hulls. You spot A-9, just as Scott emerges from the docking bay. You run up and introduce yourself, then quickly explain the situation.

"Great work," says Scott, taking the laptop out of your hands. He pulls a small diagnostic computer from his utility belt and presses it against the laptop's inbuilt processor. Next he flips a switch on his wrist communicator and makes contact with the team on Tracy Island.

"Brains," he says urgently. "What do you make of this?"

The communicator flashes up a hologram of the scientist. He is standing in his lab, screening a rolling projection of seemingly unintelligible computer code.

"The device belongs to The Hood," he confirms. "Remarkably, the data wasn't encrypted before the laptop was shut down."

"I found it on the floor," you say. "Maybe he dropped it before he got the chance?"

The both of you wait in silence while Brains scans the next chain of code. All of a sudden, he puts his hands to his head.

"Oh no!"

"What is it?"

"The Hood hasn't set up one breach, he's planted two!" gasps Brains. "The second is due to take place in just a few minutes' time. This decompression could be even worse than the first."

The engineer turns as white as a sheet, dismayed at the idea of placing so many people in danger. Scott however, remains totally calm.

"Do you have a location on the second breach?" he asks. "We need to get there and contain it, while Alan deals with rectifying the damage created by the first."

"I'm not sure," says Brains. "This code requires further analysis. I'd need to run some tests first."

Alan's voice cuts in via the communicator.

"There's no time for tests!" he exclaims. "The Estrella is tumbling towards the Earth's atmosphere. If I don't push her back into orbit soon, she is going to crash into central Florida."

Scott agrees. Quickly and efficiently, the brothers formulate a plan. Alan will start powering up immediately, then use Thunderbird 3's manoeuvring thrusters to ease the Estrella Grand back onto a safe course. You and Scott will locate the site of the second planned breach and contain the sabotage before it takes place.

"Until Brains can give us co-ordinates, we're going to have to take a call on where the breach might be and head in that general direction," resolves Scott. "Any ideas?"

If you decide to return to where you found
the laptop, go to 27.

If you think it's better to search the bulkhead,
go to 69.

32

STORY ENDS

"You're hurting me!" you protest loudly. "I'll give you the communicator. Let me turn over and I'll pass it up to you."

The man lifts his boot, allowing you to flip back onto your front.

"Who are you anyway?"

"What's in a name?" he replies, mysteriously. "I can be anything and anyone I want. Now hurry up!"

You hold out Lady Penelope's compact. But as the saboteur reaches down to grab it, you heave with all your strength and pull him down to the ground beside you. You launch yourself onto his back and hold him there. The communicator spins across the floor.

"Scott!" you bellow. "I need urgent assistance!"

The man lets out a growl of irritation. He writhes and twists left and right, furious at losing control. You struggle for what feels like an eternity. At last you hear footsteps clattering down the bulkhead corridor.

"I've got this!" shouts Scott, using a grapple pack to restrain the saboteur. He looks into the man's face, then whistles in surprise.

"Did I do okay?" you ask nervously.

"Okay?" smiles Scott. "You just caught The Hood."

THE END

33

Your head reels, trying to process what is going on. Could it be that the trouble on the Estrella Grand goes all the way up to the top? There is no injured person here – the hotel commander has been lying!

You move towards Lady Penelope, but the commander bars your way, pushing the door shut again. Quick as a flash, you stick out your foot.

"Why did you call me here?" you ask. "Release Lady Creighton-Ward at once!"

The hotel commander simply laughs. He turns his head away for an instant. When he turns back – your jaw drops. His face is completely different! All of the features seem to have morphed and changed. The youthful redheaded commander is now a dark, bald man with a brooding moustache.

"The Hood," says Lady Penelope, glaring at the stranger. "You can shift and change your disguise in an instant. But don't worry. The Global Defence Force is onto you. It's only a matter of time before International Rescue stabilizes the situation. Let this person go. This has got nothing to do with them. You'll just make things more difficult for yourself later."

The Hood disagrees. He tells Lady Penelope that you have her communicator. He has been tracking your movements ever since you caught it in the lobby!

"Give it to me," he says. "Once I have the communicator, you won't be able to make contact with International Rescue again – leaving me free to finish the job I started!"

You try to play for time, but The Hood isn't listening. He snatches the compact from you, gripping it tightly. The man deftly pushes your foot away, forcing you back into the storage unit with Lady Penelope.

"Why are you doing this?" you ask, just before he slams the door on you both. "What have you got against the Estrella Grand?"

The Hood hovers for a moment, blocking out the light. He doesn't notice another shadow looming up behind him.

"I have got nothing against the hotel," he insists. "It's what it represents. This new age in construction would mean a quick death to the industries that I have worked very hard to control. I engineered the breach. The world is watching. I want it to believe that nano-construction is dangerous, unsafe. After this, Brains' technology will be buried forever."

"You thought of everything," you reply. "Or *nearly* everything …"

You rush forward and tackle The Hood. He grapples with you, but someone else is already at his back – Parker! The bodyguard executes one quick grab and twist, instantly turning the tables. You and Lady Penelope run out of the storage unit, then trap The Hood inside.

73

"Well done, Parker," says Lady Penelope. "I wondered where you'd got to. What now?"

**If you suggest making contact with John
in Thunderbird 5, go to 57.**

**If you decide to press on and find Scott,
go to 68.**

34

"Kayo!" you urge. "Stand back."

You may not be intelligence trained, but you see instantly that the box is a highly-charged explosive. The red lights on its side begin to flicker in sequence. It must be starting a countdown.

"This doesn't look good," says Kayo, stepping backwards.

You thump a button on the outer wall with your fist and the airlock door snaps shut. The explosive is sealed inside ... for now. You and Kayo both stand for a moment in silence, pondering your next move.

There is a creak on the metal behind you. You find yourself face to face with a maintenance man holding a toolbox.

"Here to do repairs on compartment A-11," he says.

"Why?" snaps Kayo. "Who sent you?"

The man shrugs. "Just routine in-flight checks."

Kayo sends the man away. As soon as she is satisfied that the area is clear, she makes contact with International Rescue on her wrist communicator. John's hologram floats above her palm.

"You did well," he says, "but we're running out of time. We need to evacuate the Estrella before that device blows. Alan has docked Thunderbird 3 onto the hotel. He is going to load the guests into the rocket's cargo bay and get them out of here as quickly as possible. Virgil and Gordon will intercept them later in Thunderbird 2 and manage a high-altitude rescue."

"What about Scott?" you say. "And Lady Penelope?"

"Scott will be coming to meet you any second now. He will show you down to the evacuation point. Lady Penelope and Parker are already helping Alan marshal the guests onto Thunderbird 3, but they could do with some extra assistance."

You turn to look at Kayo.

"What do you think?"

Kayo narrows her eyes.

"I think there was something dodgy about that maintenance man."

**If you decide to help the rest of the Tracys
manage the evacuation, go to 18.**

**If you want to stay and track down the
maintenance man, go to 56.**

35

STORY ENDS

Panic surges through your veins. You roll and slide amongst the falling waste, trying to shield your nose and mouth as best you can.

"I feel like a tomato in a salad bowl," you groan, scouring the chute for signs of an escape route. There are none. The chute is perfectly round – a sluice shaped out of polished steel. Nothing can cling on to its sides. Every so often a blast of water gushes down the walls, dislodging any stubborn pieces of food. It seems that the only way is down.

You think of Scott in the docking bay below, wondering where you have got to. He only has minutes to get the POD in and out again before the Estrella swings back into an acute spin.

You imagine what International Rescue would do in this situation. Scott or Virgil wouldn't sit around waiting to be dumped in a refuse compactor! You begin to try and climb up and over the cascade of potato peelings, bacon rind and bread crumbs. It's a struggle to get anywhere, but after a few seconds you see another small hose pop out from the wall.

"The water spray!"

You reach out to grab the hose before it slides back again. You swipe and miss, then swipe again.

"Got it!"

You dangle by one arm, out of the rush and tumble for as long as your strength can hold. You plunge your free hand into your pocket and pull out Lady Penelope's compact. Your fingers are slippery, but somehow you stop the device from falling down into the bog of composting food.

"Scott!" you shout. "Are you waiting in the docking bay? I am slightly . . . delayed."

"Where are you?"

You hastily describe the dire predicament that you find yourself in. Quickly and efficiently, Scott asks Brains to remotely disable the waste dispatch system. You splutter in relief as the chamber floor slides back across the chute. As soon as the food settles, you let go of the water pipe and let yourself drop down to the ground.

"Thank you," you pant. "I'll come down and meet you now."

On the compact screen, Scott shakes his head.

"You missed your window," he replies. "There's no time to dock the POD now. International Rescue will handle the situation from hereon in. Goodbye, and thank you. Your part in this rescue is at an end."

THE END

36

STORY ENDS

You look up and down Thunderbird 3's cargo bay. Guests are packed in every corner – sat on laps, standing in frightened huddles, grasping on to wall fittings. You figure that Scott needs all the help he can get.

"Why doesn't Lady Penelope take the seat?" you offer. "I'll stay down here with you."

Scott passes the message to Parker. Once Thunderbird 3 has taken off, the team leader briefs you on the disembarkation procedure.

"Virgil is collecting Gordon in Thunderbird 2 as we speak. Once they are both airborne again, he will take the transporter up to its maximum altitude. Thunderbird 3 will then enter the Earth's atmosphere and stabilize its position. That's where you and I come in."

Your heart beats faster. "What do we need to do?"

"We are going to facilitate a high-altitude handover," replies Scott, passing you a spare grapple pack. "We will use these to lower the guests one by one into Thunderbird 2. Once that's complete, Virgil will get everyone back onto land. I imagine they'll be more than a little pleased to see it again."

"That sounds F.A.B., sir!" you say, nodding furiously.

Scott chuckles.

"It is," he agrees. "And no need for the 'sir'. You're part of the team now."

THE END

37

STORY ENDS

It is an instinctive reaction. You leap up, slide across the glass panel above the door and flick on its internal locking device. The knocking comes again.

"Open up, please!"

Your heart pounds. Could this be Scott or another trick from The Hood? You have already been fooled once – you don't want it to happen again. There is a third knock, and then the sound of boots on the metal floor. The footsteps finally trail away to silence.

You wait for several minutes. When you're certain that the coast is clear, you pick up the laptop and open the door. You make your way back out to the lobby. The space is crowded with guests, and a sense of panic still fills the air. Through the glass of the high window, you see a slim line of scarlet glide past. It's Thunderbird 3! You grab the arm of the nearest guest and ask her what is happening.

"International Rescue are on board," says an elderly lady clutching a handbag.

"Have you seen them?" you ask.

The lady nods. "There's a man in blue, searching each area. He's just been in the kitchens. We were told to stay calm, but my husband and I are in pieces! This isn't what we expected when we booked this holiday. I was only saying to Hank just a minute ago, we should have gone back to Vegas instead . . ."

The woman begins to chatter on endlessly, but you try to block it out. Your head throbs with an uneasy mix of adrenalin and frustration – it must have been Scott Tracy that knocked on the office door! If only you had opened it up and made contact. You take the lady's hand and try desperately to get her to focus.

"Where is he now?" you ask. "The agent from International Rescue?"

The woman shrugs, then goes back to talking about Hank and the trip to Las Vegas. Suddenly a voice interrupts her, speaking through the public address system.

"Everybody stay calm. All guests and staff should make their way immediately to the emergency zone. An evacuation is about to take place. This is not a drill."

You blink in surprise. What is going on? Has there been a second breach? Has Alan failed in nudging the hotel back into orbit? Where are Lady Penelope and The Hood? Without a direct line to Scott or the team on Tracy Island, your only option is to evacuate along with everyone else. One thing is for sure – your part in this operation is over. International Rescue will have to save the Estrella on their own.

THE END

38

Who knew that this docking bay was divided into two sections? You feel tension tingle all the way down to your fingertips. Scott Tracy is landing the POD right now. You can't waste vital seconds making the wrong choice.

"DISPATCH must be for space refuse tankers," you figure, preferring to take your chances in UTLITY. You pass through the door into a large open area lined with uniforms, tools and boots. A man in overalls approaches with a puzzled look on his face.

"Hey! You lost?" he calls. "This bay is for hotel maintenance staff only."

You try to nod casually, then duck under the man's arm. Over his shoulder you have spotted Scott in the reconnaissance POD. You sprint up to it, then climb in through the pilot chute.

"Pleased to meet you," you say. "What now?"

"We go out and examine the breach," replies Scott. "Once we've taken a molecular scan for Brains to analyse, Alan can try and push the Estrella back into the correct orbit."

"What about me? What can I do?" you ask breathlessly.

Scott pulls back a lever in the control pad above your head. "For now, hold on tight."

The POD begins to fire up its thrusters. You have never felt power like this in your life! As the craft levitates up into air, you suddenly spot the hotel commander below you, gazing out of the docking bay's viewing window.

If you decide to report the sighting to Scott, go to 15.

If you decide to stay silent and continue with the mission, go to 25.

39

STORY ENDS

You lead Scott directly up to the navigation deck, taking every shortcut you can find. Without guests and staff buzzing along the corridors, the hotel seems eerily quiet.

"After me," you say, ducking through a pair of airlock doors. Suddenly you feel someone grab your arm! Scott tries to approach, but they hold on tighter. You are shocked to recognize the smart purple livery of the hotel's commander.

"Put them down," Scott says urgently. "What are you doing?"

The commander simply laughs.

"I am taking care of the last few loose ends," he replies. He twists your body sharply, so that you can see Lady Penelope and Parker on the ground in front of you, both tied and bound, too.

"Commander!" shouts Scott.

"It is not the commander," says Lady Penelope. "We found him locked in a cupboard down in the hotel lobby, not long after the first breach. The situation really is most distressing."

The space commander begins to laugh. Suddenly his face

and body transform into a completely different person – a small man with dark, brooding eyebrows. It is The Hood, a master of disguise and ruthless international criminal.

"At last I get to meet the Estrella's saboteur," says Scott. "I should have guessed. Tell me, how did you do it?"

For the merest instant, The Hood loosens his grip. It's a do or die moment. Quick as a flash you grab the communicator in your pocket and thrust it into the man's face.

"Aaagh!" he shouts, reeling backwards.

The rest is a blur. Somehow, together you overcome the saboteur, tying him to a chair and freeing the others.

"Now if you care to follow me, Lady Penelope," you say. "We all have a POD to catch ..."

THE END

40

The box begins to make a worrying clicking sound. It must be entering the final phase of the countdown!

"We seal off this bulkhead compartment," you say, "then we destroy the device. It means another breach, but at least it will be contained."

Kayo agrees. She pushes a button on her wrist communicator, then makes contact with Tracy Island. A hologram of Brains floats above her palm, with an elderly woman beside him. He introduces Grandma Tracy.

"I like your style, kid," says Grandma. "Sometimes you've just got to go with your gut instinct, eh?"

Brains gives you a nervous nod. The scientist looks deeply troubled – devastated that his nanotechnology has put so many lives in jeopardy.

"Before you do anything, we need to make sure that everybody is evacuated safely from the Estrella Grand," he insists. "This breach might be containable, but who knows where the saboteur could strike next? Our first initiative has to be to keep innocent people safe."

"Roger that," says John, joining in from Thunderbird 5. "Alan is going to dock in the hotel's emergency zone. He and Scott will then start loading guests into Thunderbird 3's cargo bay. It's going to be the easiest way to manage an evacuation of this size."

Kayo turns to you, her eyes blazing with purpose.

"Go and help the boys load up," she says. "I can handle things here."

**If you decide to go and help with
the evacuation, go to 8.**

**If you resolve to cover Kayo's back,
go to 55.**

41

STORY ENDS

"Go after him!" you tell Kayo, pointing down the corridor. "He went that way."

"I'll come back for you," she vows.

As soon as the agent is out of sight, you pick up Kayo's laser and get to work. Brains talks to you via Lady Penelope's communicator, explaining each stage in the process. You keep one eye fixed on the pulsating grey box, racing to get finished before the device detonates. Each second feels like a year, but somehow you manage to get both ends of the compartment sealed.

"Now what, Brains?" you ask.

You look into the compact's tiny screen and observe the scientist typing furiously into a laptop.

"We need to turn the chamber into a vacuum," he says, without looking up. "I think I can do it remotely, by tapping into the hotel's ventilation programme. If my algorithms are correct, this should help minimize the intensity of the explosion. I just need one more formula . . ."

Everything that happens next is compressed into a split second. As Brains puts the last digit into his data string, there is a heart-shaking, body-shattering explosion inside the sealed compartment. Everything goes white.

The next thing you are aware of is Kayo, dragging you along the ground. She pulls you down the bulkhead corridor, towards the safety of the POD. As you get in, you notice the fake maintenance man tied up to a service pipe.

"What about me?" he shouts.

"The Global Defence Force will deal with you," she says, curtly, helping you to your seat. "Come on. Our work here is done."

THE END

42

STORY ENDS

You try the door again, but it is stuck fast. You reach down with one hand and pat your shirt pocket. Lady Penelope's compact is still tucked inside. For a fleeting moment, you consider putting in a distress call to Scott, but you abruptly stop yourself. International Rescue needs to focus on restoring the safe passage of the Estrella Grand – with or without you on the team. To divert their resources in the middle of a time-sensitive operation would be selfish. You need to figure this one out for yourself.

You probe the door again, but the lock refuses to give. A small purple pinpoint of light glints every so often, a few centimetres in from the rim. It is the only point of weakness that you can find.

You look down at the compressor one more time, then pull out your belt. The buckle is small and light, but it is made of stainless steel. You hope that it will be tough enough to do the job. You wait for the light to flash again, take aim, then hit the area with the buckle as hard as you can.

"Yes!"

The buckle damages the lock's microchip, short-circuiting the network. The door clicks ajar. You leap through the door and then clatter down a set of wrought iron steps. At the bottom is a sight for sore eyes – the bulkhead docking bay! Within seconds, Scott looms into view in the POD. You sprint across the bay and climb aboard.

"What happened to you?" asks Scott, as you throw yourself into the seat beside him. You peer down at yourself and blush. Your once pristine party clothes are now splattered with rotting eggs, mouldy vegetables and gravy. You look and smell terrible!

Scott points to a locker above your head. You reach up and find a neatly pressed blue uniform and a can of deodorant.

"You need to freshen up," he says. "And that's an order."

"I can't put this on. I'm not part of International Rescue."

"For this mission," replies Scott, "you are. So . . . let's go!"

The POD powers up out of the Estrella. It seems that your part in this adventure has only just begun . . .

THE END

43

"John," you ask, "how long can the Estrella last before the spin becomes out of control?"

"Half an hour tops," replies John. "She is on a trajectory heading down towards the Earth's atmosphere. Most crafts burn up on re-entry, but the Estrella is designed to withstand that kind of heat. Right now she's on course to land somewhere in central Florida. I don't need to tell you all how devastating that would be."

You agree, but the one thing you take from John's conversation is 'half an hour'. That should be plenty of time to fetch Brains and bring him back on board. The scientist has to be the key to putting everything right.

"We must get Brains here!" you urge. "Putting the Estrella back in orbit is only a sticking plaster – International Rescue has to stop the hotel from unbuilding itself. There are too many people on board!"

You might only be a hotel guest, but John considers your argument carefully. After a quick discussion with Alan and Brains, it is agreed. Before you know it, you are rushing up to meet Scott at the bulkhead. He takes you up to Thunderbird 3 in the reconnaissance POD, leaving Lady Penelope and Parker on the Estrella to manage an evacuation if it becomes necessary.

Stepping onto Thunderbird 3 feels strange and surreal. The highly advanced craft is like nothing you've ever seen before! Lights flash and radar screens glow with tracking data.

"Meet Alan," says Scott, directing you to a seat in the cockpit.

Alan gives you a friendly wave, then taps a joystick by his side. Thunderbird 3 veers left, down towards Earth. You are pushed back into your seat as the rocket blasts through the atmosphere and into the upper reaches of a sunny morning sky. An enormous green transporter rises up through the cloud base, then hovers directly beneath you.

"Virgil is waiting in Thunderbird 2," explains Scott. "We're going to do a high-altitude handover, so he can take me back to Tracy Island to fetch Brains."

"Let's get started," chips in Alan. "I need to get back to the Estrella."

**If you volunteer to go back to Tracy Island
with Scott, go to 21.**

**If you choose to help Alan with the next
mission phase, go to 45.**

44

You stand motionless in front of the two doors, both feet welded to the ground. The docking bay is tantalizingly close, but you had no idea that it was split into two exit ports. Scott will be manoeuvring the reconnaissance POD onto the Estrella any minute now. You have to be there to meet him!

You take a deep breath, cross your fingers, then push through the door marked DISPATCH DOCK.

It is a big mistake. You find yourself in an enormous round chamber with sliding doors evenly spaced around the edge. Every few seconds, one of the doors slides open. A massive pile of biodegradable refuse is pushed into the chamber by a robotic paddle. Another door opens, and then another. You hold your shirt over your face to cover the stench of vegetable peelings and rotting food. Suddenly you realize that you are standing in a giant recycling bin! The DISPATCH DOCK is where space refuse tankers come to collect outgoing hotel waste for recycling.

"The room is filling up!" you gasp, as more doors relentlessly open and close.

You scrabble over the growing mounds of waste, struggling to keep your head clear. Without warning, the floor slides back into the wall. The chamber is transformed into a vertical chute, taking you and everything else down with it.

"Help!" you cry, trying to avoid the crush of tumbling leftovers. You don't dare imagine where the chute will come out. One thing's for sure, however – you are in serious trouble.

**If you decide to stay compact and ride
out the fall, go to 3.**

**If you choose to try and climb back up
the chute, go to 35.**

45

STORY ENDS

You wave Scott off, then move forward to sit beside Alan. You have never flown a rocket before, but hope that your moral support will be enough to help him pull off the difficult next stage of this mission. Thunderbirds 2 and 3 diverge, streaking away in opposite directions. The velocity of travel is like nothing that you've ever experienced before.

"There's the Estrella!" you cry, just moments later.

You can see instantly that the hotel is in terrible trouble. It has tumbled even further out of the groove of its regular orbit and is now spinning wildly towards Earth.

Alan prepares his manoeuvring thrusters, then checks in with John.

"Take it steady on impact," he advises. "Advance with caution."

You look the youngest Tracy brother squarely in the eye.

"You can do this," you say confidently.

It is all that Alan needs to hear.

"First I relax," he says. "Then I don't think – I just watch and do."

He moves Thunderbird 3's joystick controller just the tiniest degree. The nose of the rocket edges towards the hull of the Estrella Grand. The manoeuvring thrusters blast, pushing up at full force. A set of fine positioning nozzles emerge from the tip of Thunderbird 3 and make contact with the hotel.

"It's moving!" you cry out loud.

There is a sudden shift, and the Estrella shunts through the inky sky, back into the correct orbit. John appears on the overhead screen, nodding his approval.

"We did it!" cheers Alan, reaching out to give you a high-five.

You settle back into your seats, then watch Thunderbird 1 emerge from above the horizon. Brains is on board, ready to pit his mind against The Hood and save his latest creation. You have a pretty good hunch that he's going to do it, too. No situation is too desperate for International Rescue!

THE END

46

"Eeny, meenie, miny mo, catch a villain by the toe."

You choose the right entrance, wondering anxiously what might be waiting for you in the bulkhead corridor. Could the saboteur be hiding there, planning their next move? You shudder at the thought.

You begin to run in the opposite direction to Scott, using the flashing map inside Lady's Penelope's compact to guide you. At this pace, it doesn't take long to get to the entrance. When you reach the agreed marker, you crouch down against the corridor wall and talk into the communicator.

"Scott," you say urgently. "Are you ready to seal off the breach. I'm good to go ..."

Suddenly your voice breaks into a strangulated cry. A bald man with menacing eyes lurches out of the shadows, then effortlessly trips you.

"Give me the communicator," he says politely. "I don't want you to chit-chat all day to International Rescue. You can talk to me instead."

The man pins you on the floor. The saboteur has got you right where he wants you …

If you decide to hand over Lady Penelope's communicator, go to 32.

If you are brave (or foolish) enough to resist, go to 50.

47

STORY ENDS

Now you know for certain – there is definitely a saboteur at work on the Estrella Grand! You push on to the escape bay as fast as you can in zero gravity, with Parker and Lady Penelope gliding closely behind. Vital seconds tick by. At last you turn a corner and spot the red and white warning lights signposting the hotel's emergency zone.

"The door is locked!" you shout urgently.

Lady Penelope turns to her bodyguard.

"You know what to do, Parker."

Parker nods, then pulls a tiny explosive out of his top pocket, no bigger than a coin. He swiftly fixes it to the airlock handle.

"Stand back, M'Lady."

It only takes the touch of a button to detonate the door. *Bang!* You move into the bay with your ears still ringing. As you take stock of the scene, things do not look good. Every single escape capsule has already been dispatched from its launch pod, bar one at the very end of the row. You make your way over to it.

"This is not going to solve our problems," you sigh. "The capsule has room for fifty people at most!"

A maintenance worker opens the cockpit window and waves you away.

"This one has a malfunction," he shouts. "It won't be going anywhere."

You grimace at Lady Penelope. You've wasted valuable time getting down to the bay ... all for nothing. John makes contact one last time.

"The Estrella only has minutes before it falls through Earth's atmosphere," he presses. "We have to abort. Alan is docking in the port below you. Your job now is to gather the hotel guests and help them load into Thunderbird 3's cargo hold. Scott will meet you shortly to assist. Once all the guests are on board Thunderbird 3 and out of here, Virgil will intercept with Thunderbird 2 and initiate a high-altitude handover. Is that clear?"

"Crystal," replies Lady Penelope.

"But what about the Estrella? If that crash lands on Earth it could cause all kinds of destruction. I have to find who did this and put it right!" you shout.

John Tracy's voice goes quiet.

"I'm sorry," he mutters. "You just ran out of time."

THE END

48

STORY ENDS

You slowly edge yourself out of the recess and back down the corridor, one footstep at a time. As soon as it is safe to do so, you make contact with Scott.

"Don't move a muscle," he says firmly. "I'll seal off the right entrance to the bulkhead, then work my way round to you."

You creep back to your vantage point. The figure is bent over now, and you can hear the echoing sound of tools working – maybe a laser or a micro-drill.

"I'm here," whispers Scott, just a few minutes later. You move on together, spreading yourselves across the width of the corridor in order to block off any escape routes.

"Kat?"

You step round the bend and see the young reporter that you'd been watching earlier in the hotel lobby! Kat Cavanaugh glares at you, her eyes blazing with anger and panic. She tries to run, but you tackle her to the ground.

"Look Scott," you say urgently. "She's working on another breach."

You point down to a small grey box with flashing lights along one side. Scott scans it with his wrist device.

"Not yet activated," he confirms.

"It would have been!" blurts out Kat. "If you hadn't interrupted me."

Scott gives you an appreciative high-five.

"Let's seal this corridor off," he says. "Once the area is safe, we can analyse the technology in this box and find out who this young lady is working for. Good work, you did a great job."

THE END

49

STORY ENDS

"We have to destroy the box," you shout. "We can worry about the saboteur later."

"Too dangerous!" insists Brains. "If the device explodes, the breach will cause a catastrophic decompression."

Kayo nods grimly. "You, me and everything not bolted down will be sucked into space within nanoseconds."

You think of the hundreds of innocent passengers on board and instinct takes over. You dart forward and pluck the box off the wall. The flickering lights on its side become an ominous red flash.

"So we'll just have to make sure that it doesn't explode," you say, tearing back down the corridor. Kayo flicks her wrist communicator off, then sprints after you.

You jump through the airlocks, scanning the bulkhead walls.

"The garbage chute. There!" barks Kayo.

You lift up the lid and fling the box down, hoping it will skim, not bump, against the chute walls. Finally you hear an explosion go off ... in the void outside the Estrella. Kayo is seriously impressed.

"Now we've just got to find the saboteur," she says, giving you a high-five. "Are you ready?"

"I'm ready for anything," you grin. "Thunderbirds are GO!"

THE END

50

STORY ENDS

"No," you say firmly.

"No?"

The man is surprised, outraged even. He furrows his brow, checks himself, then tries again.

"Resisting me really would be very foolish," he says, "but then you don't know who I am."

You turn the communicator over in your palm, wondering what to do. While the saboteur talks, you secretly slide your nail under the rim of Lady Penelope's compact and open it a touch.

"No," you reply loudly. "I don't know who you are. I don't usually rub shoulders with criminals."

The man is so affronted, he seems to forget about the communicator. You lift it closer.

"I'm not a criminal!" he scoffs. "If only you knew the power I had at my fingertips! Who else would be able to unravel the mysteries of nanotechnology? Who else would be able to take over an entire space hotel singlehanded?"

"Wow. Now that *is* powerful. I wouldn't expect anything less ... from The Hood."

Scott looms up behind the saboteur, alerted by your conversation over the open comms line. The Hood recoils, but he has left it too late to escape. From this point on, International Rescue, with your help, is in control of the Estrella Grand. Good work!

THE END

51

STORY ENDS

Your heart sinks. Resisting the tip of the floor is getting harder and harder. Very soon you are going to find yourself in the jaws of the compressor. This is rapidly becoming a life or death situation.

Gingerly, you use one hand to root around in your pocket. You find Lady Penelope's compact and prise it open with your thumb and forefinger. You daren't take the device out and look at the screen – it would be too easy to lose.

"Scott!" you shout. "Can you read me?"

There is a moment of silence . . . and then the faint sound of Scott's reply. You quickly explain the situation. Within seconds, International Rescue has located your whereabouts in the dispatch dock.

"Hold tight," says Scott. "I am going to station the POD in the bay, then seek you out on foot."

He is true to his word, but it is a slow and difficult rescue. When you finally see Scott push through the chamber door, many crucial minutes have passed.

"What now?" you ask expectantly.

Scott frowns.

"Too late," he replies. "Our part in this mission has been aborted."

THE END

52

STORY ENDS

You feel a dull thump somewhere far below you, then the navigation deck lurches. The Estrella rights itself slowly back onto its intended course. You steady yourself and then wait for the confirmation from John.

"Well done, everyone," he says finally. "We're back on track."

You and Lady Penelope resume your places at the control board, ready to guide the hotel through the next stage of its journey. Suddenly Brains appears on the communications screens. An elderly lady in a purple jumpsuit is standing in the lab beside him – Grandma Tracy.

"No further action required," he says. "I have managed to reverse the molecules' self-destruct impulse! The Hood's formula took a while to decode, but when I experimented with quantum theory and ..."

Grandma Tracy cuts in.

"Yes, yes, yes Brains ... all you need to know is that you're safe. You and everyone else on the Estrella! I am going to make cookies to celebrate."

Suddenly you catch Grandma Tracy's eye.

"Have *you* tried my cookies?" she asks, peering at you over her glasses. "My boys love them! I'll bake you a batch right now ..."

You gulp. What Grandma can't see are the Tracy brothers on their comms screens behind her, shaking their heads and pulling faces.

"Only the boldest recruits can stomach one of Grandma's cookies," whispers Parker. "Best of luck to you!"

THE END

53

STORY ENDS

"Be careful," you say, reluctant to leave Scott to search the hotel alone.

He gives you a quick smile. As the eldest Tracy brother and the natural leader of International Rescue, he takes high-pressure situations in his stride. Scott has been staring danger in the face and saving lives ever since he can remember. Before you say another word, he runs off towards the main elevator shaft.

The public address system switches its message, just as you climb into the last escape capsule and click your safety harness into place.

"Capsules are ready to depart. Prepare for launch."

One by one, the capsules shoot out of the emergency zone exit hatch. You lean forward to look out of the window. The Estrella Grand looms magnificently in the darkness below you – a vast floating city ready to explore the furthest corners of the Milky Way.

"She was built for a great future," you sigh, taking one last look. "Shame it had to end before it had even begun."

The escape capsule increases velocity, using its thrusters to tear itself out of the Estrella's orbit. Soon you and the other guests are being told to brace yourselves – as the craft prepares to re-enter the Earth's atmosphere.

The capsule is small and compact, but it rocks with the turbulence. The mood on board is tense and uneasy. You grip the handles of your seat, clinging on with grim determination until you see the domed curve of the Earth come in to view. A woman in the row behind you taps you on the shoulder.

"Where are we going?" she asks. "How will we get home?"

You try to reassure her, but you have no idea how to answer her questions. Blue sky appears and then a blanket of cloud. The escape capsule plunges into the cloud and out the other side. Below you, all you can see is ocean.

"We're going too fast!" you whisper to yourself, as the capsule continues to fly through the air at terrifying velocity. You wait for its re-entry parachutes to be released – vital for creating air resistance. Nothing happens. Instead, there is a sudden impact, followed by darkness. You have landed in the sea.

The other passengers begin to shout and cry, despite your efforts to keep everyone calm.

"There was a small malfunction with the capsule's parachutes," you explain. "But don't worry. International Rescue are supervising this evacuation. They'll be here soon."

You turn yourself towards the window, then flip open Lady Penelope's communicator. A cheerful looking blonde guy instantly shows up on the screen.

"Gordon Tracy," he says amiably. "I have been tracking you. My squid-sense was tingling!"

"Where are we ... and where are you?" you wonder.

Gordon checks his co-ordinates, then breaks into a wide grin.

"You are sinking in an escape capsule just off the eastern coast of Florida," he replies. "And me? Luckily myself and Thunderbird 4 just happen to be in the neighbourhood, too! Please tell the passengers that everything is going to be okay."

You turn back to the lady behind to you, but there is no need to say a word. Everyone in the capsule is cheering already! Somehow all of you voyaged in the Estrella and made it out alive.

THE END

54

You cannot refuse the hotel commander. You run to his assistance, hoping that International Rescue will understand the reason for the delay.

"Quickly sir," you urge. "Show me the way."

The hotel commander's face instantly brightens. Curiously however, instead of taking you back out towards the lobby, he shows you through the main kitchens towards a huge storage unit at the back. The hairs on the back of your neck suddenly stand up. Something doesn't feel right.

"Who is hurt?" you demand. "Where are they?"

The hotel commander turns a wheel set into the wall. The massive iron storage door slowly swings open. You gasp in surprise. Lady Penelope is standing inside, her hands bound in front of her.

"It's a trap!" she hisses. "Run!"

If you decide to do as Lady Penelope says, go to 28.

If you have the courage to stay and challenge the hotel commander, go to 33.

55

"I'm not leaving you to deal with this," you insist.

Kayo puts her hands on her hips. At the moment she sees you as a liability. You need to show her that you can be an asset.

"By the time I get down to the emergency zone, the evacuation should be winding up," you tell her firmly. "I may be just a hotel guest, but at least I'm *here*. We don't currently know who or where the saboteur is. They could be hiding in the next corridor! You seal the compartment. I'll watch your back."

Brains' hologram has remained silent . . . until now.

"It's a compelling argument," he adds. "You should agree, Kayo."

"Do what Brains says," agrees Grandma. "Get the job done together, then get out. You could be back on Tracy Island by teatime. Tell you what, Kayo – I'll even make you some cookies."

"Okay, okay!" says Kayo, bringing the conversation to an abrupt end. "No need to make cookies, Grandma. I'll start sealing the south end of the compartment. You can keep watch."

You do as you are told, your heart racing inside your chest. For several minutes there is nothing to see. You scan the compartment corridor. Over your shoulder you can hear Brains talking Kayo through the sealing process. First she uses a portable electronics jammer to override the automatic airlocks. Next she produces a small handheld laser from her body harness. A faint smell of burning drifts along the corridor as the metal melts around the entrance frames.

Tip-tap. Tip-tap. Tip-tap.

What was that? You run to the end of the corridor and come face to face with a hotel maintenance man.

"Evening," he says brightly. "Just doing routine checks in area A-11."

"No need. I just saw one of your colleagues working in A-11. I reckon he beat you to it."

You try to make your voice sound casual. After all, you don't want to worry the guy. The man looks puzzled for a moment, then his face breaks into a toothy grin.

"Looks like my tea break has come a few minutes early," he says amiably. "See you!"

The maintenance man picks up his toolkit and disappears back down the corridor. Silence returns. That's when you catch your breath

"Kayo!" you whisper urgently. "I think we have company."

Kayo shuts down the laser and runs over. You tell her about the mysterious maintenance man.

"He looked genuine," you admit, "but who carries out routine maintenance when there is a mass evacuation taking place? All the guests and staff should be making their way onto Thunderbird 3!"

Kayo listens intently. That's when she tells you about The Hood. The man is an international tycoon, captain of industry … and a wanted criminal. He is also a master of disguise.

"I don't know why he would want to hijack a space hotel," she muses, "but he has to be dealt with. He could be on his way to set up another device right now!"

If you volunteer to go after The Hood, go to 9.

If you decide to focus on containing the breach instead, go to 41.

56

STORY ENDS

"John," you say firmly. "We may have a lead on the saboteur. We've got to check it out."

"No time," frowns John. "Thunderbird 3 is scheduled to be airborne again in two minutes!"

"I still have the POD," says Kayo, pointing at you. "We can use that to escape when we're finished."

You turn away, so that Kayo can't see you blush. It looks like International Rescue has accepted you as part of the team!

"Tell Scott to go back to the evacuation point," you insist. "We'll deal with the saboteur!"

John signs off. As his hologram fades to nothing, a flicker of doubt runs down your spine. You hope that you are doing the right thing.

Luckily there's no time to dwell on it. Kayo flicks off the communicator, then leads the way back along the bulkhead.

"There he is!" you shout, pointing to a figure kneeling next to the outer wall.

You surround the maintenance man and demand to know

what he is doing. The guy seems flustered, bewildered even. He holds out a screwdriver and a neon light bulb.

"Light blew in this recess," he shrugs. "Been sent up to change it."

You can barely hide your groan of disappointment.

"You better come with us, sir," says Kayo, helping the man to his feet. "There's an evacuation going on. If we are very lucky, we *might* just make it."

Wrong call, rookie. You tried to help out International Rescue, but you've still got a lot to learn!

THE END

57

"The situation is changing fast," you say. "We need to talk to Thunderbird 5."

"Quite right," replies Lady Penelope, reaching for her handbag. Parker coughs politely, then passes her the silver compact.

"Ahem. You forgot this, M'Lady," he says. "I took the liberty of relieving The Hood of it before I shut the door."

Lady Penelope's face lights up.

"Oh Parker. I don't know what I'd do without you."

Lady Penelope flips open the compact and checks in with Thunderbird 5. The interior of the comms hub is buzzing with activity. John floats between virtual screens, analysing data and processing surveillance feeds from all over the world.

"Alan is about to attempt a manual adjustment to the Estrella's flight path in Thunderbird 3," he confirms. "We need to get the hotel into a safe orbit. Scott has surveyed the breach in the reconnaissance POD. Unfortunately the information that we're getting back from the molecular data scan is not looking good."

"What's up?" you ask.

John touches a screen, bringing up a large infographic of the Estrella Grand.

"The Hood hasn't just damaged the fabric of the ship – he has instructed the component molecules to 'unbuild' themselves. The hotel structure should be indestructible by normal means, the molecular bonds are just too tight. Whatever The Hood has done has upset the polarity of these bonds. The consequences could be catastrophic."

Your heart pounds. It looks like the hotel is on a course for self-destruction ... with everybody on board!

"I trust that Brains is looking for a solution," says Lady Penelope. "This is his technology, after all."

"Brains is trying to source the infiltration, but he's reaching the limit of what he can achieve remotely," replies John.

"We need to get him here," you insist. "On board! Can Alan go and pick him up?"

John shakes his head. His first priority for Thunderbird 3 is to nudge the Estrella back into orbit. You are not so sure.

If you decide to go with John's analysis,
go to 16.

If you want the Tracy brothers to get Brains
onto the Estrella, go to 43.

58

STORY ENDS

Carefully, quietly, without arousing suspicion, you tuck one hand into your shirt pocket and flip open Lady Penelope's compact. There is an almost imperceptible click as the comms line activates.

"Why do it, Kat?" you ask, hoping that Scott is listening. "All this just to land a bigger story?"

"It appears that Miss Cavanaugh has an interesting side-line," says Lady Penelope.

The reporter smirks. You discover that she is on the payroll of the consortium of scientists publically discrediting Brains' nanotechnology. His new construction methods would mean the end of the industries that they operate.

"When the Estrella goes down, she will take the future of nano-construction down with her!" declares Kat.

". . . or perhaps not." replies a voice behind you.

Scott appears in the doorway. He walks up and shakes your hand.

"Sorry for the delay," he smiles. "I was just busy detaining the hotel commander. Now if we could all make our way to the reconnaissance POD? The Global Defence Force would very much like to meet Miss Cavanaugh."

THE END

59

STORY ENDS

"We have to get that data!" you insist, pointing towards the breach.

Another rock clatters against the POD's hull.

"Not possible right now," says Scott. "We'd both get pummelled to smithereens."

"Not if we did the molecular scan from the *inside* of the hotel," you suggest. "Go back down into the bulkhead docking bay. I can lead you on foot to compartment A-9."

Scott begins to smile.

"Brains," he says, touching base with Tracy Island. "Does that plan work for you?"

"Affirmative," replies Brains. "We have to get that data!"

Scott moves fast, landing the POD before it takes on any more collateral damage from the meteor shower. As soon as you are back on board the Estrella, you lead him back to the bulkhead corridor.

"We are near the breach," you say.

Scott is right behind you. He clamps his handheld molecular scanner against A-9's compartment wall and turns it on. The device gathers everything it needs in under three seconds.

"We've captured the data!" says Scott, reporting back to International Rescue. "Sending now."

John's hologram appears above Scott's wrist communicator.

"Great work," he says. "Are you ready for phase two?"

Scott glances across at you.

"Are you in?" he mouths.

You reply with a short, determined nod.

"Team ready," he confirms. "Let's do this!"

THE END

60

"Somebody certainly wants Brains' technology to fail," frowns Lady Penelope. "The question is what do we do about it?"

"Let's split up," you decide. "You and Parker go check out the escape bay. I'll head up to the control deck. Maybe I can stop the saboteur before they cause any more trouble!"

Parker raises an eyebrow. He leans forward and whispers something in Lady Penelope's ear.

"I appreciate that they're untrained," nods Lady Penelope, speaking into the communicator, "but we are rather short on resources. What's your take, John?"

"Affirmative. Two teams are better than one," replies John. He looks you firmly in the eye. "Go to the control deck now. Scott is trying to gain access to the hotel's starboard dock. He'll meet you up there."

You wave goodbye to Lady Penelope and Parker, then move towards the first exit you can see. You feel lost without the communicator. You remember being shown around the Estrella's impressive command suite when you first arrived, but which floor was it on?

You pick your way along corridor after corridor, time rushing through your fingers. At last you find yourself outside the central elevator system. You climb inside, then stare blankly at the monitor panel. Which floor do you choose?

If you press the button for the top floor, go to 23.

If you opt for the button marked HOTEL PERSONNEL ONLY, go to 66.

61

You try to think clearly. Slowly and deliberately, you scan the lobby. Your eyes pass over the teeming reception area, across the dance floor and through to a gleaming, neon-lit cocktail bar. At the very back, you can just glimpse a small service door reserved for waiting staff only.

"It must lead to the hotel kitchens," you guess.

It takes all your energy to float towards the bar. You try using your arms and legs to swim through the air, but soon realize that it is quicker to grab onto furniture and fittings, then haul yourself along. Weightlessness feels strange, disorientating. Any slip in concentration sees you somersaulting up towards the ceiling.

When you get to the dance floor, you pass the space hotel commander, besieged by frantic guests all demanding an explanation.

"There's been a small decompression in bulkhead A-9 through B-10," he tells them in shaky voice. "There really is nothing to worry about. We'll have it contained in no time at all."

You move on, slowly picking your way through spinning chairs, cocktail glasses and tumbling ice buckets. When you finally make it to the bar door, it opens automatically to let you through. You find yourself floating in a small airlock. When the next door opens, you drop to the floor like a sack of potatoes. You realize that the kitchens are sealed, protected from the decompression affecting the communal areas of the Estrella Grand.

"Shame," you mutter, "I was just getting used to my 'space legs'."

You find a quiet corner away from the kitchen staff, then open up Lady Penelope's compact. You hastily introduce yourself to John and the rest of the Tracy team.

"We're on to it," confirms John. "The decompression has pushed the hotel out of its orbit. The crew is reporting that some of the manoeuvring thrusters were damaged in the blast. They can't control the spin."

"What now?" you ask.

"We need to get the hotel back into a stable orbit," confirms John. "Scott and Alan are on their way in Thunderbird 3. Alan will use the rocket's thrusters to push the hotel back into position."

"What about me?" you urge. "I can be of assistance! I've been exploring the hotel for 24 hours – I know my way around already."

"I'm not sure . . ."

John frowns. International Rescue is a highly trained, elite organisation. The Tracy brothers haven't worked with outsiders before – they've never needed to. You press the point, determined to be the first.

"Scott," asks John. "What do you think?

An image of Scott flashes up on the compact screen. He is now sat beside Alan in the cockpit of Thunderbird 3.

"If the Estrella does not get back into orbit soon, it is going to enter the Earth's atmosphere and crash. The results would be catastrophic," he says grimly. "I'd say that we need all the help we can get."

It is agreed. You listen carefully as John briefs you on the next steps. As soon as Thunderbird 3 reaches the Estrella, Scott will leave the rocket in a reconnaissance POD.

"Make your way to the bulkhead," he says. "I'll meet you in the docking bay near the entrance to compartment A-9."

You repeat the plans back, then sign out. The bulkhead is up at the top of the ship, so you'll have to go back through the lobby to get there. As you run back towards the airlock door however, someone comes through from the opposite direction. You recognize the smart purple livery of the hotel's commander.

"Please help me," he says. "Somebody's hurt!"

**If you decide to stick to John's mission brief
and press on, go to 6.**

**If you feel choose to stop and help the hotel
commander, go to 54.**

62

You race back towards the space hotel's kitchens as fast as your legs will carry you. You heart pounds harder with every breathless step. Finally you leap through a set of automated doors, back to the place where you last saw Parker. You duck and dash past the Estrella's legion of fridges, worktops and ovens. At the far end of the kitchens, you spot the chrome storage unit where Lady Penelope had been trapped. You wonder what happened when Parker appeared to disturb The Hood's plans. You hope that the saboteur is now the one being detained. You can't even contemplate any other outcome.

"This is it!" you mutter, rushing forward and flinging open the storage unit door.

It is empty. Lady Penelope, Parker and The Hood are nowhere to be seen.

Your plan is in free-fall. You need to get that laptop to International Rescue! You begin to furiously search the kitchens – looking into storerooms, staff bays and vast walk-in freezers. You approach an office marked HEAD CHEF. You step inside, closing the door behind you.

Something has happened here. The monitor screens on the wall are cracked, chairs have been pushed over and the head chef's personal effects have been spilled over the floor. Suddenly there is a knock on the door. You freeze.

"Open up, please!"

If you decide to open the door, go to 2.

If you decide to operate the internal locking system, go to 37.

63

STORY ENDS

In a crisis, plans have to shift and change to keep up with unfolding situation. The new priority has to be getting the Estrella out of this meteor shower and back into orbit.

"Let's go back to Thunderbird 3," you say urgently.

Scott doesn't need to be asked twice. The POD shoots away with breathtaking speed. Within seconds the craft is docking back into Thunderbird 3's cargo hold. You follow Scott into a transport chute that whisks you both right up to the cockpit.

"Take a seat," says Alan, gesturing over his shoulder.

The ride is much smoother up here. Thunderbird 3 has a magnetic force field that automatically repels meteors, defunct satellites and other space junk. Alan explains that he is about to manually shift the Estrella back into orbit.

"Firing up thrusters now," he says. "Get into brace position."

"Anything I can do to assist?" you ask, eagerly.

Alan chuckles, but shakes his head.

"Thanks, but International Rescue will take it from here. You're in safe hands."

Your heart sinks. If anyone can save the Estrella, it will be International Rescue. You just wish you could do more now. Scott gives you a friendly pat on the shoulder.

"Never mind," he says, "at least you get a front row seat."

THE END

64

STORY ENDS

"The box is on a countdown," you shout. "I vote that we get out of here now!"

"Copy that!" shouts Kayo, breaking into a run.

You tear through the bulkhead corridors side by side, determined to put as much distance as possible between you and that explosive. You don't stop until you make it back to the airlock door.

"What is it?" demands Kayo.

"If we can seal this airlock up properly we might be able to contain the breach," you reply breathlessly.

Kayo eyes up the airlock. It is programmed to open automatically whenever it detects pressure on the corridor floor. In order to lock it shut, you will need to manually override the circuit. You decide to go for it.

You use brute force to keep the airlock shut, while Kayo tampers with the door's control pad.

"Hurry!" you urge, sweating with the effort of holding the door.

Kayo only needs a few seconds.

"Done!" she says, just as a massive explosion knocks you both to the ground. The device has detonated – the sheer force of the impact is heart-stopping! You glance over at Kayo. Somehow, you are both still alive.

You flip open Lady Penelope's compact.

"John?" you say. "We contained the breach. What next?"

John smiles. "Spoken like a true member of International Rescue!"

THE END

65

STORY ENDS

Vital seconds are ticking by. You have to do something. You scan the shelves behind Lady Penelope and Parker, then spot a metal blowtorch hanging from a hook. It's a small, antiquated object, but a kitchen essential. The chefs on the Estrella use the tool to get a crisp burnt topping on crème brulées and other fancy desserts.

You leap forward and snatch the torch down, then press the wrist grip. A flare of heat bursts out from it. Kat flies at you, then jumps back.

"Stand there!" you shout, pushing her into the corner of the room.

Somehow, keeping one eye on the reporter, you are able to use the blowtorch to melt the lock in Parker's wrist restrainer. As soon as he pulls himself free, Parker moves in to apprehend Kat.

"You're coming with me, Miss," he says. "The Global Defence Force will be wanting a word with you."

"Why did you do it?" you ask.

139

Kat scowls. Lady Penelope explains that the reporter has been working undercover for the consortium of scientists trying to discredit Brains' nanotechnology. She was due to earn millions, but all she is in for now is a spell in prison.

You help Lady Penelope get free, then hand back her precious silver compact.

"International Rescue cannot thank you enough," she says solemnly.

Your chest swells with pride.

"Now let's go and find the hotel commander," you reply. "We'll pick up Scott along the way."

THE END

66

STORY ENDS

You press the button labelled HOTEL PERSONNEL ONLY. In an instant you are transported up to the very top of the Estrella Grand. The doors open and you find yourself floating in a corridor that leads to staff quarters, a vast media centre and a honeycomb of offices. Right at the very end is an airlock door – offering backstairs access to the control deck.

You open the airlock and go through, relieved to find yourself back in a normal pressurized environment. A man with piercing blue eyes strides towards you. It must be Scott – commander of Thunderbird 1 and the eldest Tracy Brother! He reaches out to shake your hand.

"Thank you for your help," he says briskly, leading you through to the mainframe computer at the epicentre of the control deck. "Brains is working on finding the source of the breaches right now."

A hologram of Brains appears above the computer in front of you. The engineer looks troubled, his brow furrowed into a deep frown.

"The molecular structure of the nanomatrix has been unzipped. Someone has found a way to instruct the component molecules to 'unbuild' themselves. But how? I need more data urgently! Scott, did you have any luck locating the hotel commander?"

"Negative," replies Scott.

You think back to the Estrella Grand's lavish opening ceremony.

"He was in the lobby just a while ago," you say. "I saw the journalist, Kat Cavanaugh, interviewing him."

"But Kat is over *there*," replies Scott. He points to a woman with a mic in her hand, badgering the commander. She must think it's her lucky day – the only press on the scene of a breaking major disaster!

You approach them, determined to ask a few questions of your own. The commander scowls, then turns on his heels and makes a dash towards the exit.

"Quick!" you bellow, throwing your hands around him. To your astonishment, he slips away from you, transforming into a sinister looking man with a bald head and glowering dark eyes.

"The Hood!" declares Scott. "I should have known that you would be behind this."

You and the stranger lock eyes, circling each other like caged animals. The man appears menacing and dangerous. He is also clearly a master of disguise.

"What have you done with the hotel commander?" you press.

The Hood sneers at you.

"Tied up and taped up in his office," he announces, breaking into mirthless laughter. "Once I'd blackmailed him into giving me his access codes, I was free to hack into the mainframe computer. It was almost too easy! I've planted devices all over the hotel – breach after breach after breach!"

"I'm impressed," you say. "Tell me more."

The Hood can't resist. He takes you through each step of his plot, explaining his actions in careful, grim detail. He's too engrossed to notice you discreetly signal to Scott behind your back.

"... by the time I'm through, Brains' nanotechnology will be finished," he winds up at last.

"Not quite," you say, turning to the mainframe computer. "Did you get that, Brains?"

Brains' hologram beams at The Hood.

"Every last detail," he replies. "You gave me all the data I needed to disable the breaches and reinstate the nanomatrix's self-repair protocols."

Scott pats you on the back.

"Good work!" he grins. "F.A.B.."

THE END

67

You pick up the pace, climbing higher and higher up the ladder. As you float pass the portholes, your jaw drops at the sheer size of Thunderbird 3 flying alongside the spinning space hotel. A panel slides open on the side of the rocket and a mechanical grappling arm appears, locking itself onto the Estrella Grand. There's a blinding flash of light as Thunderbird 3's thrusters power up. The rocket must be preparing to push the Estrella back into orbit! You picture Alan Tracy inside the cockpit, carefully guiding the craft through the heart-stopping manoeuvre.

"Look outside the window, Lady Penelope!" you shout desperately. "I can help you."

Lady Penelope floats elegantly off the top rung of the ladder, then dusts down her trouser suit. Parker glares at you.

"All right," she says. "Who are you?"

As soon you get to the top, you introduce yourself and hand over the compact.

"I've been speaking to International Rescue," you whisper urgently. "We have a situation!"

Parker steps in front of Lady P, then grabs you by the collar. "Shall I take care of this, M'Lady?" he says in a gruff voice.

"No thank you, Parker," she replies, smiling at you sweetly. "You have 30 seconds to explain."

You breathlessly tell Lady Penelope how you retrieved her compact and raised the distress call when the space hotel fell into free fall.

"I am loyal. I can keep a secret," you urge. "Let me help save the Estrella!"

Lady Penelope finally drops her guard. Something in your face has convinced her to trust you. She shakes your hand then introduces herself as International Rescue's London agent. Niceties out of the way, she makes contact with Thunderbird 5. John Tracy appears in her compact screen.

"What are our instructions?" Lady Penelope says. "Is Alan having any success in forcing the Estrella back into orbit?"

"Negative," replies John. "There has been another breach to the space hotel's nanomatrix. I think it's time to get the guests aboard the escape capsules. If the damage isn't fixed soon, the hotel will crash through the Earth's atmosphere."

Parker taps on the porthole. A steady stream of capsules are flying out of the space hotel already.

"They must be empty," frowns John. "Someone has triggered the manual override!"

If you decide to press on to the escape bay,
go to 47.

If you decide to ask John for a Plan B,
go to 60.

68

STORY ENDS

"We have to hurry," you insist. "I am meeting Scott near the source of the breach. Thunderbird 3 is going to attempt to stabilize the Estrella and push it back into orbit."

Lady Penelope is impressed.

"Lead the way," she replies.

Lady Penelope and Parker follow you back into the lobby and up through the hotel. Within minutes, Scott Tracy is striding towards you, his eyes filled with purpose.

"Alan is on standby," he says, "but first we need to check that there are no further breaches along this bulkhead. Another decompression could be catastrophic for the Estrella."

You work as a team. Together you sweep every compartment along the bulkhead corridor, scanning for signs of damage in the structure of the ship.

"We're good," you announce at last.

"Okay," nods Scott. "Let's get the POD back to Thunderbird 3."

You glance over your shoulder towards Lady Penelope and Parker, then realize that Scott is talking to you.

Soon you are taking your seat in the Thunderbird's cockpit, just behind Alan Tracy. Alan turns back to shake you firmly by the hand.

"So it looks like International Rescue has got a new recruit," he grins. "Let's do this!"

THE END

69

STORY ENDS

You try to steady your thoughts – with stakes this high you can't afford a wrong move.

"Why would The Hood be doing this?" you ask Scott. "Why is he interested in the Estrella?"

"It's got to be the hotel's unique nano-construction," he replies. "The Hood wants to discredit it permanently. He controls a huge chunk of the world's technology, but if Brains' cutting edge new science works, most of The Hood's industries will be eclipsed and made redundant."

"... but to put all of these lives at risk!"

"That isn't The Hood's usual style," admits Scott. "Knowing him, I'd guess that the civilian passengers are more of an unnecessary by-product. His main focus will be to ruin the future of nano-construction. And what could be a better way of doing that than for the Estrella to endure a disastrous maiden voyage? The whole world will be watching!"

You take another step or two along the bulkhead.

"I vote we start here then," you say suddenly. "Right now!

The breach was in compartment A-9. If I were The Hood, I would focus on causing as much damage as I could in one area. If the decompression is more intense on one side of the ship, it would make the spin more lopsided and out of control."

Scott agrees with your theory. Together you make your way along the bulkhead corridor, moving methodically from compartment to compartment. Sections A, B and C reveal nothing. Then you get to compartment D-6.

"Over here!" you shout, pointing at a small grey device with red lights running up the side. It has been placed on a high cable ledge, just out of eye-line.

Scott gives a short, sharp nod. You have found the second breach! When you step towards it however, the ship lurches to one side, throwing both of you to the floor. The device slides off the ledge and clatters further down the compartment.

"Is that Alan?" you shout, wincing every time the device bangs across the metal grille floor.

"Correct," replies Scott. "That shunt was Thunderbird 3's fine positioning nozzles pushing the Estrella Grand back into orbit. Looks like it's been successful, too."

You blink in surprise. The hotel does seem to have righted itself. Instead of moving in a lurching spin, the motion is even and steady. You and Scott creep deeper into compartment D-6. The lights on the device synch then start to flash.

"It must be a countdown," you say breathlessly. "We have only got seconds ..."

Scott makes one last urgent contact with Brains.

"We have located the breach," he says. "What now?"

Brains' hologram is surrounded by swirling strings of

formulae. You notice that his hands are trembling as he scans the endless rows of numbers.

"D-d-d-data is just coming through ..." he stutters.

"Hurry!" you shout.

Brains finally reads out a numeric code – 7 3 6 8 2 9. Without thinking, you sink to your knees beside the device and press the numbers into the keypad on its side. The box blinks furiously for three seconds ... and then stops. Scott puts his hand on your shoulder.

"Congratulations," he says with a smile. "You just saved the Estrella Grand."

THE END

70

STORY ENDS

"This way!" you bellow, leading Scott out through the maintenance area and into the bulkhead corridor. The hotel commander cannot be in two places at once. You are convinced that the man in the viewing window has to be an imposter.

You run in single file down the empty corridor towards compartment A-9. As you round the final bend, Scott leaps in front of you, throwing you back into a recess on the left hand side. He puts a finger up to his mouth to tell you to stay silent.

You nod in understanding, then peer over Scott's shoulder. A man in a purple uniform is standing just metres away, connecting cables to a small grey box. It must be another breach!

"Hello Commander," says Scott, stepping out of the shadows. "Shouldn't you be down on the navigation deck? The hotel is in a terrible spin."

"International Rescue. I wondered when you'd drop by."

The man doesn't seem surprised. Instead he steps towards

you both. As he does, his disguise slips away in plain sight. You watch transfixed as the figure transforms into a slight, bald man in a tailored suit. Scott introduces you to The Hood – the most notorious technology thief in history.

"We've located our saboteur," says Scott. "And it's all down to your quick-thinking. Great job. International Rescue will never forget this!"

THE END

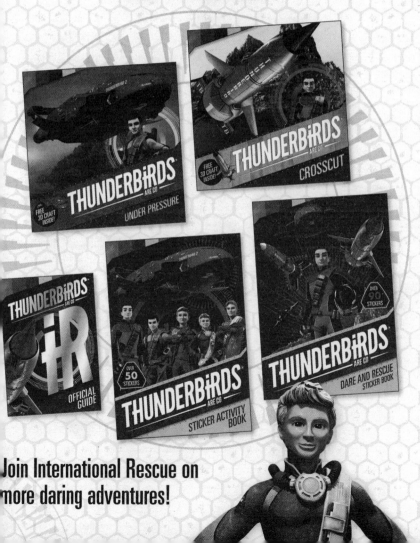

THUNDERBIRDS ARE GO

LOOK OUT FOR THESE OTHER AWESOME THUNDERBIRDS ARE GO BOOKS
OUT NOW!

Join International Rescue on more daring adventures!